The Beast Beside Me

The WOLVES of WHARTON
Book One

THE
BEAST
BESIDE ME

BEAU LAKE

4 Horsemen
Publications, Inc.

4 Horsemen
Publications, Inc.

4 Horsemen Publications, Inc.
1497 Main St. Suite 169
Dunedin, FL 34698
4horsemenpublications.com
info@4horsemenpublications.com

Typesetting by Michelle Cline
Edited by Vanessa Valiente

Audio ISBN: 978-1-64450-202-0
Paperback ISBN: 978-1-64450-204-4
Ebook ISBN: 978-1-64450-203-7

DEDICATION

For M, para siempre.

TABLE OF CONTENTS

———◆◇◆———

PROLOGUE
(JAMES)

———⊲♦⊳———

I discover him amidst the crush of bodies. Our hands accidentally touch, my knuckle against his thumb. His eyes are a deep brown, like the bark of a Douglas Fir. "Hey," I say, taking a slow slug of the bougie Stout I had ordered. Babe Brau is Le Creme's crown jewel; a dark, thick sludge named after Paul Bunyan's ox, featuring a shirtless bear-like lumberjack on the label.

It's vile, but it's dollar beer night. I want to get fucked up. I've had a horrible day.

"Hey," he parrots, nearly shouting over the crowd and the pop music pumping through the speakers, the bass making the floor thrum as if alive. "God, you're fucking gorgeous."

No matter how many times I hear it, the compliment still makes me preen.

Angus would hate this.

No, don't think about him.

I laugh, leaning close. "Can I buy you a drink?" When he nods, delighted, I take him by the arm, steering him toward the bar. He's handsome, but that's not what piqued my interest. His scent reminds me of a succulent ribeye steak, my favorite meal at RingSide Steakhouse. I typically pair it with a Pavillon de Léoville Poyferré, an old-world red with notes of cedar.

It's an earthy meal, reminiscent of the fare consumed by hunters and gatherers. If it weren't for the linen tablecloths and candlelight, I could imagine myself squatting on my haunches, gnawing on the meat, and lapping at the wine as thick as blood.

He orders an Old Fashioned, and we clink glasses. The beer in my bottle froths, the foam thick and cream-colored. I can't help but touch him, resting my palm on his hip, hooking my finger through his belt loop. He blushes a deep crimson and licks his lips.

"Dance?" he asks, his lips brushing against my ear.

"I don't dance," I reply, but I tug on his belt so that our hips briefly touch. His breath hitches.

He rests his palm against my chest. "Drugs?" he offers.

"Absolutely." We finish our drinks, and he takes my hand, leading me toward the bathroom. We skirt around a queen freshening up her makeup, drawing a thick swoop of eyeliner on her glittery lid. There is one free stall, and we wedge in together.

He fishes inside his pockets and pulls out a small baggie, a one-third of white powder.

"What's your name?" he asks me. "I'm Ronnie." Ronnie taps a line of powder onto the only available surface—the screen of his iPhone. Jostled, the screen brightens, and I catch a glimpse of Ronnie, his arm wrapped around a lascivious blond with darkly contoured cheeks and pursed lips. *His girlfriend? A sister?* It doesn't matter. I don't really care.

"James," I reply, watching as he sniffs a line. He wrinkles his nose, rubbing his nostrils with the heel of his hand. I take the bag from him, tipping a small bump out onto my knuckles and inhaling it. My sinuses go numb, and my neurons sizzle.

"Mmm, James," Ronnie purrs, his fingertips drifting under the hem of my shirt. His lips press softly against mine. "I like that name." His eyes dilate into black voids.

"You smell *so good*," I say, pressing him back against the plastic laminate stall. He feels so different from Angus' sharp edges and taut sinew. Ronnie, conversely, is soft, succulent. He enthusiastically rubs my cock through my jeans with his palm. He thinks it's flattery, a compliment. It is, but not in the way he thinks. "Want to get out of here?" I ask, nipping at his lower lip.

He winces. "Okay," he replies thickly. "My car is in the parking garage at the end of the block. We can go to my place. It's in *Forest Park*."

He's bragging. He may as well have announced his net worth.

Ronnie shoves the baggy of coke into his pocket, then brushes his phone screen with his shirttail. Together, we return to the club proper, winding our way through the crush of bodies and undulating limbs. A Lady Gaga song plays, and hundreds of voices scream-sing along with Mother Monster.

It's cold outside, a chilly drizzle peppering our hunched shoulders. After the heat inside the club, it feels like a slap. "I don't usually do this," Ronnie says. "Invite someone home, I mean."

"Yeah?" I'm not listening, not really. I'm not quite sure what I intend to do. When we are in private, am I capable of pushing Angus out of my mind so I can kiss those wet lips, giving into my impulses to go further? Despite the effect of the coke, my confidence falters. Angus' angry facade materializes in my mind's eye. His pale face in the window appeared like a phantasm of the past, of what I intend to rip asunder with my teeth.

After this, there's no going back. Angus was very clear about that.

Ronnie's car is on the ground level of the concrete parking structure. The sounds of our nearly synchronous footfalls echo through the enclosed space. "This one's mine," Ronnie announces, tapping a button on the key fob he's magicked from his pocket. *Beep*. It's a black Mercedes-Benz SUV. Sandwiched between Ronnie's car and the sedan beside it, Ronnie grows impatient, kissing me hard. He really does smell *very* good. I kiss him back, cupping the back of his neck. His tongue slithers into my mouth. "I don't think I can keep my hands off of you," he whines.

So be it. I open the back door, pulling him inside with me.

Wedged together in the backseat of his car, we paw at one another. He straddles my lap like a teenage girl after prom, desperate for her stammering date to put his hands under her skirt. Methodically, I press my thumbs into the dimples at his hips, running my knuckles along the sharp ridge of his ileum. With his shirt shucked up around his midsection, I can just make out the tuft of platinum hair above his low-slung waistband.

"What's your name again?" he asks, his fingers tangling in my hair. His hot breath smells faintly of citrus. His voice has a raspy quality to it, probably from nearly yelling in my ear at Le Creme, droplets of his spittle flecking my cheek.

"James," I remind him. *He's more inebriated than I thought. Or perhaps, more stupid.* I try not to think of Angus waiting for me in our shared apartment. *You're impossible,* I'd said, before I slammed the door shut, before I got onto TriMet toward Burnside Triangle. I hadn't planned to walk into Le Creme, and I certainly didn't plan to rut in a stranger's car.

"I'm Ronnie," he breathes, the tip of his tongue drawing a languid circle on my neck. With his body this close, his smell is intoxicating; the hair prickles on the back of my neck.

"I know," I reply, unbuckling his belt and threading it through the loops. *And I don't care*, is what I want to tell him. It's like asking a cow's name before pressing the bolt gun against her wide forehead.

I suck his lower lip between my teeth, making him gasp. Ronnie lifts his hips so I can push his jeans down his muscular thighs. His cock strains against his underwear, a moist spot of precum wetting the fabric. When I pull the waistband down and stroke him, he nearly seizes with excitement.

Humans are so fucking malleable.

"You're so *good*," he groans. When his head tilts back, saliva pools in my mouth as I watch his jugular pulse. *God.* Angus will never forgive me if I do this.

I can apologize for my angry words, but there's no apology for what I'm doing, nor what I'm about to do.

"I feel like I'm fucking stagnating!" I growl, throwing Angus' legs off my lap. The muted beiges and blues emanating from the television screen flicker across Angus' handsome face as he surveys me wearily. "We're more than this, Angus."

"What do you mean?" he asks, startled by my outburst. "Would you rather watch something else?"

"We shouldn't be doing this." I gesture around the room as if to encompass everything therein. Angus' blue eyes follow my hands: our bed with its dark navy bedspread, the stainless-steel Nespresso machine sitting in our kitchenette, and the black-and-white photos on the walls of us, the pack, and the Portland skyline. Domestic. Fucking. Bliss. My resentment bubbles in my stomach, crawling up my esophagus like bile. I can't swallow it; it burns. "You desperately want us to be something we're not."

Angus bristles. He tries very hard to appear unstirred, but I can see it in the stiffness of his jaw, the dark indent just below his ear. "We decided—"

"You decided," I cut him off. "You decided, Gus, and I'm fucking miserable." I reach for my jacket, slinging it on over my thin tank. I don't want to be here, pacing back and forth like a tiger overcome by his captivity. I'm tired of looking at my cage, figurative or otherwise. Conversely, I don't want to say something I'll regret. Instead, I let the words sit on the back of my tongue.

Angus rises. "What would you have done?" He's smaller than me, in both height and breadth, but he is intimidating all the same. Even in this form, he is as immovable as a tree, all sinew and vigor, rooted by his convictions. Do no harm, he says, we are not above anyone else. But aren't we? Shouldn't we be? Are we not apex predators?

"What we've done for thousands of years," I snap, smoothing the jacket's collar against my neck. "Running, eating, fucking. Anything."

Angus releases a short, hollow laugh. "And where do you expect we do that? In the Shanghai Tunnels while we scratch our fleas?" *he asks, referring to the old trafficking tunnels beneath the city.*

That's his problem; Angus never sees the bigger picture. If we desired, we could force the humans to shelter in the Tunnels, force them to cower when they hear our heavy footfalls on the asphalt overhead. We could take our place in both lexicon and legend.

"We could eat our fill, like our forefathers and -mothers," I snap. "But you won't even hear it. You are so damn ashamed of what you are."

"I'm not ashamed," *he insists as he steps closer and touches my elbow.* "Come on, James. You know we can't live like that. This isn't the fifteenth century." *His words bring images of our kind loping through the woods to mind, our fur fiery in torchlight. 'Loup, loup!' shout a cacophony of voices, driven mad by the sight of their countrymen ripped apart, limb from limb.*

"You shouldn't be Alpha," *I say, jerking my arm away from him. At first, I want to take back my words— the secret thought I silently mulled over in the dead of night—and punch them down my gullet. But then, no! I'm tired of stewing, gritting my teeth, hating my mate even when he kisses my lips.*

"Excuse me?" He leans close, his hot breath on my face. "Are you challenging me?"

"No." I laugh. "Keep your shitty, little pack. I don't want it." Angus' face contorts, and for a brief moment, his teeth elongate, filling his mouth. I've rattled him, and it feels gloriously satisfying. "I'm done," I whisper.

"And me?" he asks, unable to mask the hurt in his voice.

"Yeah." I open the front door, stepping out into the hall. "Even you," I say as a parting shot. "You're impossible."

As I stroke Ronnie's cock, my fingernails thicken and grow. The telltale paresthesia tickles my belly and chest as fur erupts from my pores. Ronnie is entirely unaware of my metamorphosis, his eyes half-lidded and vacant with ecstasy. He presses his palms against the Mercedes' ceiling, his limbs cast upward as if thanking god for the touch of my hand. He doesn't notice as my toothy grin elongates into a snout, tendrils of slobber dangling from my canines. With my wolven nose, his smell becomes all the more irresistible. *I need him. Now.*

With my free hand, I smack Ronnie sideways, his skull striking the windowpane with a muted thud. "Wha—" he manages, before I am on top of him, my bulk taking up the majority of the space. Bizarrely, he tries to pull his pants up, but can't. He's woozy from the blow to the head, and his hands are shaking terribly.

Ronnie looks up at me with one rolling eye and starts to scream. We are parked in the darkened corner of a parking garage with only one flickering fluorescent bulb above. I must look like something from a horror movie. *The Wolf-Man Cometh!*

"Goodbye, Ronnie," I say, my voice glottal yet piercing. Then, I clamp my jaws over his neck, splintering his vertebrae. The screams stop, and for a moment, there is only gurgling. Then, blissful silence.

His blood coats my tongue, and I sigh with delight. It tastes just as delicious as I imagined, metallic and somewhat briny. His flesh is akin to pork, and I like the fattier parts the best. His ass, round and pale, is particularly tender. Eating human flesh surpasses the cocaine high tenfold. Before this, I've only eaten woodland animals, though that was a rarity. Angus thought it was uncivilized, but conversely, wouldn't pay for the privilege of eating in a Michelin-starred establishment.

He certainly wouldn't go to RingSide Steakhouse with me. That was something I did *alone.*

I want to eat more, but my stomach is uncomfortably full and distended. Satiated, I shrug my wolfishness off, the pain of my transformation just barely lapping against my parietal lobe. I'm naked now, my clothes stretched and torn at the seams in my haste to consume Ronnie. I clamber over the center console, leaving smears of blood and viscera, and ease into the plush leather driver's seat. I stretch like a cat sunning on a windowsill. I've never felt so *good,* so content.

Ronnie had tossed his keys and wallet into the passenger seat as we tumbled into the back, our limbs tangled together. I casually open his wallet, intending to pocket any cash, but the name on his driver's license gives me pause. Ronald Nedry III. *Where have I heard that name before?*

CHAPTER ONE
(ANGUS)

———⊲◆⊳———

We abandon the car in Ohio.

After twenty-three hundred miles, we pull into a Marathon Gas in Finley, eager for a respite from the cramped sedan. In the dark, my eyes blurry with fatigue, it's difficult to keep the dashed center line from meandering. Once we've safely parked, I rest my head against the headrest, shutting my eyes.

The doors open and close as my passengers stretch their legs, using the bathroom and shopping for over-priced snacks. Only James stays in the car, curled up in the backseat.

He pants, and the sound lulls me to sleep.

"Heads up," Luka murmurs, sliding into the passenger seat. "We have company."

I crack my eyelids open and glance out the driver's side window. Several spots away, a police cruiser idles, the officer leaning against the hood. He sips from a Styrofoam cup, idly watching our car. A warm trickle of adrenaline edges down my cervical spine.

"James," I hiss at the wolf in the backseat. "Keep your head down."

He doesn't reply, his rhythmic panting seemingly interminable. He's unbothered.

The officer catches my eye, and gestures for me to roll down the window. I glance around for Leigh, and see her topknot bouncing between the aisles inside the store. *Shit*. I roll down the window. The officer gestures at our car, cup in hand. "What breed of dog is that? He's enormous."

"Just a mutt," I reply, my voice remarkably even.

The officer sidles closer, peering through the glass. James, to his credit, tucks his nose under his bushy tail, making himself as amorphous as possible. There's no feasible way he can be mistaken for a dog, especially viewed this close. His body is more humanoid than wolf-like. We run upright, though we are digitigrades like our canine cousins. Our bodies are uniquely designed for it: long limbs, thick haunches, and torsos reminiscent of a malnourished fox during winter.

"Where are y'all coming from?" the officer asks.

Luka leans over me, flashing the officer a grin; it's too wide and artificial. "West coast, sir." His voice is artificial too. As a black man, he is all too familiar with the dangerous dance we are now partaking in.

His eyes meet mine and his smile widens. *Smile*.

The door chime *bing-bongs* as Leigh exits the shop, her arms full with a drink carrier with four coffees inside, and family-sized chip bags tucked under each armpit. She is blissfully unaware of the tense situation and sets the drink carrier on the car's roof as she tosses the chip bags onto Luka's lap. "Sorry," she says. "I had to wait for the guy to brew a fresh pot of coffee." Then she notices the police officer. "Oh!" she exclaims.

The officer's hand rests on the pommel of his sidearm. I can't tell if it's a habit, or if he sees us as a threat. We must look suspicious; three adults, stinking and exhausted, their car's floorboards littered with receipts, empty coffee cups and crushed energy drink cans. "You have four cups there, miss," he observes coolly.

Leigh looks at the drink carrier, still oblivious. I can almost see her doing arithmetic in her head. *One, two, three, four. Leigh, Luka, Angus... James.* Leigh chuckles. "It's a vice," she replies. "I get terrible migraines without it."

She hurriedly tucks the drink carrier into the car, spilling a bit onto Luka's lap. Then, she opens the back-door and slides in, absently patting James' furry flank.

The officer is still looking at our car. I give him a little wave, hoping he will return to his cruiser. "Y'all have a good night," he finally says. But he doesn't return to his car. Instead, he mounts the curb, glancing at our license plate before waving goodbye.

"Fuck," I breathe as I pull away, flicking on the blinker to merge onto the interstate. Once the gas station is out of sight, I smack my palm on the steering wheel. "Fuck!"

Luka wordlessly hands two coffees back to Leigh. James sits up, his fur melting away. "We would have looked far less suspicious if I had been human," he scoffs. When his keen claws finally transform into nimble fingers, he takes the coffee from his twin sister. With his free hand, he searches for his discarded

3

clothes beneath the driver's seat, bumping my chair as he does it. I want to *throttle* him.

"There's a description of you," I snap, glaring at him in the rearview mirror. We've had this discussion before. And now, the officer has the license plate of a car registered to Angus *fucking* Chilton, whose live-in boyfriend matches the exact description of a person-of-interest.

"In Oregon," he snorts.

"There shouldn't be a description of you *at all*." I pull off at an exit, steering into a quiet neighborhood. There are very few streetlights here, so I park in a pool of inky blackness, then remove the key from the ignition.

"What are we doing?" Luka asks.

"Everyone get out," I prompt.

"Angus——" James' tone is exasperated. But he's been annoyed since we started this troublesome road trip. He *thinks* he's untouchable.

"Out," I repeat.

"Angus, you aren't—" Leigh starts.

"Get out of the fucking car!" I open the driver's side door and step out into the street, slamming it shut behind me.

James rolls down the window of the ancient Nissan. "Get back in the car, Gus." It's his nickname for me, reminiscent of sweet kisses on rooftop bars or entire days intertwined in bed. It just *pisses* me off.

Within moments, I step into my wolfish form and reach into the window, wrapping my claws around James' neck, then wrenching his still-naked body from the car.

"Let go," he gurgles, kicking at me with his feeble, human feet.

I let go, dropping him into a heap. "We're running," I snarl.

♦ ♦ ♦

We run parallel to the seemingly endless highway, careful to keep the cacophony of engines and concrete Jersey barriers on our left. We head toward the East Coast, skirting around cities, loping through quiet townships. I used to have dreams like this, running beyond exhaustion until my paws go numb and my heart resonates like a bass drum. I used to think the dreams meant I had a case of wanderlust. But now I know otherwise.

I was dreading the inevitable.

It's autumn, and I'm glad for it. In two more months, when the first snowfall coats the Shenandoah mountains, we wouldn't survive the journey on-foot. I lead the way, my ears pricked forward and my nostrils flaring, searching for a familiar scent. We're getting close now. And then, *there!* The smell of salt and something else, something far less pungent calling to me like a siren's song. *Home!*

Luka lags behind, his tongue lolling from his mouth. But now that we're nearly there, I can't stop. I don't dare; *will the smell fade away, towed upward by a rogue thermal?* And if it does, *will I find it again? Almost there,* I mime encouragingly with only a yip and a flick of my ears. Leigh slows to nip at Luka's ebony flank, spurring him onward. Shoulder-to-shoulder with me, James grumbles, the sound deep in his throat. I want to *bite* him.

We wouldn't be running if it weren't for him. I think longingly of our converted warehouse, the plush cocoon of my duvet, running through the velvety darkness on the Eastbank Esplanade, drinking at Hubers, and seeing obscure jazz bands at Rimsky. I want to look out my window at the skyline—find the blue-gray smudge of Mt. Hood on the horizon. I even almost miss the old pipes groaning whenever we turned on the faucet or ran a shower; the water was always bitterly cold. I even miss my job at the hospital, being lulled into a stupor by the centrifuge's calming hum.

From the corner of my eye, I look at James, trying very hard not to admire his long, slender snout, or the way his powerful shoulders are freckled with charcoal and slate. When he runs on all four paws, his muscles ripple like ocean waves. When he stands upright, his haunches bulge.

Remember. You're supposed to hate him, I try to remind myself. Yet still: I do miss rolling over in bed and kissing the valley between his shoulder blades.

It's just past midnight, and James hasn't returned home. I peer out the window, searching for him in the warm glow of the streetlights. But, it's all for naught; despite my constant vigil, the narrow alley between the warehouses remains empty.

We had a fight before he left.

"You shouldn't be Alpha," he snarls before he slammed the door shut. As he stomped down the stairs, I wanted to follow him. Instead, I watch out the window as he pauses beneath a streetlight, lighting a

cigarette, his shoulders taut. A stray cat approaches him, weaving between his legs, but he nudges it away with the toe of his boot. Then, he noticed me watching him. The cigarette dangling between his lips, he raises his arms as if to say what now? *But I just shake my head and turn away.* There's nothing else to say.

I sit on the couch, pull my laptop onto my lap, and scroll through my email inbox, deleting hundreds of accumulated ads. The process is somewhat soothing: click, delete, click, delete. Eventually, I doze, chin to chest.

The apartment door bursts open, and James nearly falls through it. He's naked, bits of twigs knotted in his mussed, greying hair. He's been wolfish. There's a tacky, dark substance on his chest, his arms, his chin, even his thighs. Blood. The smell is cloying, coppery and thick. It makes me feel heady. Saliva pools in my mouth—a reflex—but I swallow it down.

I put aside my laptop and rise from our threadbare couch. "What happened?" *I ask, resting my hand on his heaving chest. His heart is a staccato under my palm. That is what I find most alarming. James is* never *shaken.*

"He's dead," *James replies, his voice devoid of emotion.*

"Who?" *I ask, pulling James close and burying my nose into his hair. He smells like cedar, smoke, and—*

I jerk away from James as though he's punched me in the gut. He smells like someone else. He sleeps in my bed, but he smells like someone else. "Who were you with?"

7

"I fucked up, okay?" James brushes past me, padding barefoot into the kitchenette, leaving smudges of red on the linoleum. He rips a handful of paper towels off of the roll, shoving the whole lot under the faucet and wipes blood off his face, pink trickles edging down his bearded jaw. "I couldn't stop myself," he continues. "I couldn't stop."

"Who was it?" Despite the blood and his harried appearance, I can't stop thinking about him touching someone else.

"It doesn't matter who he is," James mumbles. He lurches toward the fridge, pulling out a beer and unscrewing the cap. He chugs it, his Adam's apple bobbing. I want to slap it out of his hand. "What matters is that he's dead, and they'll search for who did it. Turn on the TV, Angus."

While he scrubs the clotting blood off his hands, I search for the remote. My skin feels tight; it takes a tremendous amount of restraint not to give in to my more predatory nature. I want to squeeze his windpipe until his face turns crimson, purple, then finally, grey. I find the remote under the couch cushion and turn on the local news.

A weatherman, his mouth stretched into a toothy smile, pushes a cartoonish cloud over Portland. Then, he announces a commercial break.

"Maybe they haven't found him," James says hopefully, sinking down onto the couch beside me. His naked thigh presses against mine, and I scoot away. It's a childish thing to do, but I don't care.

"You fucked someone else," I remark as we watch a Swiffer mop commercial.

"We aren't together anymore, remember?" James replies coolly, picking at the label on his beer bottle.

I scoff. We broke up hours ago.

Before I can reply, the Channel 7 News logo cuts into a Tampax commercial. "Breaking news out of Burnside Triangle," announces the coiffed anchorman. "A man, identified as Ronald Nedry III, has been found dead. The police are ruling it a homicide..."

I am wolfish before James can react. We both tumble to the floor, but, in this form, I am far heavier. My jaws tighten around his throat. He grasps at my muzzle, trying in vain, to pull my jaws apart with his weak, human hands. The man he killed is well-known in the city of Portland: an entitled playboy and the son of the mayoral incumbent.

Killing him was stupid. So, so stupid.

The click of cameras and a familiar voice forces me to release him, returning my attention to the television screen. "What happened to my son is a tragedy," the mayor says, his eyes dilated from the flashbulbs, his lips trembling and pale. "If anyone has any information, please contact the Multnomah County Sheriff's office." He ignores the pleading of the press pool ("Mr. Mayor, Mr. Mayor!") and steps off-stage, slipping out of sight.

James wriggles under my heavy paw. "They clearly don't have anything, we're okay—"

The Sheriff steps up to the podium, clearing his throat with a phlegmy cough. "Nedry was last seen at Le Creme, a gay bar in Burnside Triangle, talking with a man described as Caucasian; early to mid-forties, salt-and-pepper hair, heavily tattooed with a broad build. We want to speak to this man, who is, at this time, a person of interest." While vague that description is unmistakingly James. A thought bubbles up out of the mire of my rage and sadness: we have to go.

The Sheriff continues, "The state of the decedent's remains are unusual..."

We run for another fifteen minutes before the trees thin and the lights of a small, seaside town dot the horizon. I haven't been to Wharton in two decades, and it has changed as much as I have. But the bones are still there. I can see the cylindrical water tower, the town's name painted on the convex exterior. The letters, once painted in a bold, cheerful gold, are now indecipherable smudges on the weathered surface. While I can't see them, I hear the waves breaking on the barriers flanking the pier. I used to climb the tetrapods as a young teen, the rough concrete hot under my palms and the soles of my feet. I long to enter town proper and search for my old haunts. But first, I must find my grandmother.

I lead the way, descending a steep hill, mindful of loose rocks underneath my paws. James hangs back to watch out for Leigh and Luka. That's okay; I don't particularly want to be near him, either.

On even ground, I press my snout to the ground, inhaling. I can smell her; it's faint, but it's unmistakable. She smells so much like me; our fur is the same. I follow the scent to a small bungalow on the shoreline, the front yard littered with beachy paraphernalia: a crab trap, two folded beach chairs, and a towel draped on the porch rail to dry. On the porch, a metal pinwheel slowly turns, creaking. It's an affront to my sensitive, wolfish ears.

Suddenly, the front door bursts open, and the screen hits the wall with a resounding slam. A frail woman pumps a shotgun, aiming it between my eyes. "Who are you?" she asks.

I step out of my wolfish form and rise. "Granny," I call, holding up my hands. "It's Angus." I'm stark naked, but neither of us seem to notice nor care. Nudity is common amongst wolf folk.

"Angus?" she steps off the porch, her rubber boots squelching in the dewy grass. Ama Chilton is far shorter than me, and she has to stand on her tippy toes to squint at my face with watery eyes. Her gray hair is tucked behind her ears, and I can see a hint of her wolfishness therein. Her ears are slightly pointed and tipped forward, giving her a pixie-like quality. When she grins, her teeth are jagged and sparse. Old age is hard on our kind; it becomes far more difficult to control the transfiguration from wolf to man, then back again. Most end up somewhere in-between, but *most* don't live as long as Ama has.

"Yeah, Granny," I reply, touching her papery-thin cheek. "It's me. We need a place to stay—a safe place." I gesture to my packmates. Leigh's fur melts away and she hugs herself, gooseflesh spreading on her breasts and forearms. James and Luka follow suit.

While he tries to look unruffled, Luka's lips tremble. Six months ago, he was bitten by a lone wolf passing through Powellhurst, so every transformation still agonizes him. Even after thirty-six years, my muscles burn. I must grit my teeth as my haunch contorts into a hip.

"You haven't visited in ages," Ama accuses, albeit a gentle one.

"I know," I say, trying to appear suitably chagrined. "Can we come in?"

Ama looks pointedly at her neighbors' bungalows, the windows dark and the curtains drawn closed. "I suppose," she replies. "I don't want the neighbors thinking I'm running some sort of brothel."

She steps up onto the porch, leaning heavily on the wobbling bannister. The pack and I follow.

The interior of the bungalow is cramped, filled to the brim with antiques and books, smelling faintly of mold. Despite the clutter, the space exudes warmth. The furniture is plush and piled high with crocheted throw blankets. The shaded lamps emit a honey-colored glow.

"Have a seat," she says. "I'll put the kettle on and see if I have any spare clothes." She shuffles into the kitchen, and I hear the tap running, then the teapot clanging against the sink.

"She seems nice," Luka remarks, sinking into the sofa. His jaw stiffens into a right angle as he absently runs his fingers over his locks.

"Are you okay?" I ask as he worries one of the thick tendrils with his fingers.

"Yeah, man," he replies, waving away my concern. "That's the longest I've ever been *him*." We all have our own words to differentiate between our human and wolven selves. While we are still undoubtedly *ourselves* in either body, wolfishness is akin to drunkenness. In that body, we are far more uninhibited, driven by our gurgling stomachs and our yearning flesh. "It was hard to remember who I was," Luka continues.

"It'll get easier," Leigh assures him. She sits in an Edwardian-style armchair, crossing her long, pale legs. "Before I got it under control, I'd wake up in Laurelhurst Park, covered in duck feathers."

James loiters in the doorway, a hulking mass of a man. We haven't been human in eight days, and I am unprepared for the wave of turmoil washing over me at the sight of him. He is broad and muscular, his arms thick, his hands calloused. Road-weary, his shoulders slump and his hair is stringy. "Why here?" he asks gruffly.

We've already discussed this. It's as though he thinks asking again and again will temper my resolve. "We're safe here," I say slowly. "Wharton is small, rustic. They probably haven't heard the news."

"Heard what?" Ama returns, her thin arms laden with an assortment of clothes. She drops a paisley stretch of fabric into Leigh's lap. Leigh holds it aloft to reveal a humongous, sleeveless muumuu, with thick cording around the chest. "Sorry dear," Ama apologizes. "All I could find was my old maternity dress."

Leigh laughs, slipping it over her head. The neckline is wide, revealing both her shoulder cap and the curve of her clavicle. Despite the dress's grotesquely loud pattern and poor fit, Leigh is still radiant. Being waifish affords her such luxuries. "I'll make it work," she assures my grandmother. "Thank you."

Luka is given a pair of too-short sweatpants, and a t-shirt from the local diner-cum-motel: the Wharton Great Inn. "Thanks," he grunts, pulling them on. Ama gives his shoulder a squeeze as if to say, *everything is okay.* She has always been a stalwart presence in my life and seeing her interact with my packmates is proof of the power she has over others; she is the salve we so badly needed.

"Here you go, Aggie." She hands me a wrinkled dress shirt and a pair of worn jeans. "These were your Papa's," she says, referring to her late husband. "Hopefully, they'll fit. You always were his mirror image."

"Aggie," James chuckles, but she doesn't seem to hear. She merely pushes a corded sweater and a pair of dress slacks into his arms.

"Now," she says, clapping her hands together. "Someone answer my question. Who heard what?"

"We had to leave Portland—" I begin.

"We didn't have to leave," James grumbles, cutting me off.

"We had to leave Portland," I repeat through gritted teeth. "Because we got into some trouble."

"'We,'" Luka scoffs. Ama sits on the couch beside Luka, resting her hands on her knees. Her large, blue eyes focus on me.

"James killed someone, left evidence, and I made the decision for us to leave," I say, choosing to be matter of fact rather than continuing to beat around the bush. Clearly, no one had found that approach favorable. I also don't want her to be cognizant of the deep divisions in my pack. It's embarrassing. I'm meant to be in charge, but a man died.

And no one sees me as the leader I should be. *I'm floundering.*

Somewhere, in the depths of the bungalow, the kettle whines, escalating to a sustained screech. Ama doesn't move to remove it from the burner, so the unsettling sound fills the space, lancing through my ears.

"You brought a murderer into my home?" she asks, her voice even.

I don't know what to say. I glance at James, who pointedly avoids my eyes. "I didn't know what else to do," I manage, sweating under her heated gaze.

"In my day, we would have eaten them," she snaps. Her eyes slide toward James, the corner of his lip twitching as he stifles a laugh. "Don't you dare smirk at me. Or, I'll eat you *now,* pup."

"We can stay somewhere else," I say quickly. "Just until we decide what to do next."

"How much do the humans know?" she asks. But she's not looking at me, she's looking at James.

"They only have a vague description from a few witnesses. My hair color. My tattoos. Nothing more." He pushes up his sweater sleeve, showing off the ink on his forearm. The sight of the cursive "A" on his ring finger makes my stomach turn. The commensurate "J" on my own *now* feels like a brand, a reminder that we are still married. Even if we divorced, he'll still be omnipresent.

He touched Nedry with that hand, *hadn't he?*

"Do they realize how he died?" she asks. The kettle's squeal continues, unabated. None of us dare turn it off. Granny is holding court. Despite her frailty, she is the strongest among us, the only anchor to our past, a cruel world that James holds up as an ideal.

James sits on the armrest of my chair, his hip brushing against my arm. I can't help but to wrench my arm away. *Don't be a petulant child,* I silently admonish myself. "I'm not sure. The last headline I saw insinuated that he was brutalized, but there was no mention of an animal attack. They made several references to Ed Gein, so I suppose they think I'm wearing his entrails as a belt."

Ama presses her pale lips together. "If you are staying here, there will be absolutely no recklessness. At the very first mention of a wolf attack in Portland, you will continue on. I am far too old to deal with your juvenile nonsense."

"Okay, Granny," I murmur.

Leigh and Luka verbalize their consent.

James just shrugs, wearing his bravado like armor.

CHAPTER TWO
(HUNTER)

◁◆▷

I relish waking up early, just before the sun edges above the horizon.

I leave my bungalow before the seagulls have taken wing, their small gray-and-white bodies tucked amidst the beach grass. Taking a detour down the pier, my footfalls echoing on the planks, it's as though I'm the only person in the world. The ocean is dark and slow-rolling, muted by the dense fog that typically accompanies the sunrise here. The moist air beads on my hair, wetting the back of my neck.

When I finally trundle down Main Street, the sky is pink, and I am no longer the sole resident of Wharton. The teenage newspaper deliverer rides past on his bicycle, the wheels squeaking rhythmically. Eddie, the owner of Seaside Books, pushes a book cart onto the curb in front of his store. A yellow sign exclaiming BOGO! flutters. "Hey, Hunter," he calls with a congenial wave. "G'morning."

"Trying to move those Pattersons, huh?" I ask, gesturing to the cart full of heavy volumes.

Eddie shrugs. "He's prolific, what can I say?"

"Put the ninth Alex Cross book aside for me, will you? I just finished *Four Blind Mice*."

"Of course," he says cheerfully. "You can pay me with a coffee. Maybe a bagel, too." He adjusts his BOGO sign, his lips pursed as he concentrates.

My cafe, Ebb and Flow, is three doors down from Seaside Books. I unlock the door and step inside, tossing my keys onto the countertop. I take the chairs off the tabletops, tucking them under the small cafe tables. Then, I switch on the equipment, fill the caramel, chocolate, and hazelnut syrups, make a large batch of whipped topping, and brew a carafe of coffee.

Finally, I grab a handful of chalk markers, and head for the curb to write on my easel. It's my favorite task. I like writing cute sayings like *Good Days Start with Coffee—and You!* Today, I settle on *Sweet Dreams Are Made of Cheese* with a sloppy rendering of our baked brie pastry.

"Hey, boss," mumbles a sleepy voice from above. Renee rests her elbows atop the A-frame, looking down at my handiwork. As usual, she wears a hoodie that is too large for her frame while her dishwater-blonde hair is pulled into a messy topknot.

"Hey," I say, rising after I put the finishing touch on my drawing: a plume of steam rising from the savory dessert. My knees ache. "How was your night?"

Renee fishes a pack of cigarettes from the kangaroo pocket of her hoodie. "Oh, you know. Same old, same old." She lights a cigarette, taking a long drag. "Stagnating."

I chuckle. Renee is only nineteen, and Wharton is far too sleepy for her. "We open in fifteen," I remind her. "You're on register." Her groan follows me inside.

I trot into the backroom and find Emmanuel placing piping hot croissants onto cooling racks. He's been here for hours, baking and prepping today's fare, and his workspace is flanked by a carafe of coffee and a jug of water.

"Still trying to drink all that in a day?" I observe.

"Yeah, and I piss every five minutes," Emmanuel grunts, not bothering to look at me, too engrossed in his work. I can just barely see the blown-out edge of the teardrop tattoo underneath his eye. His apron is untied, and tangles around his thighs as he works. But he doesn't pause to fix it.

He reaches for black and white frosting bags, defrosting on the counter. "The black-and-whites are a little well-done today," he says, gesturing at the nearby rack of soft cookies with his elbow. The edges are a little more brown than usual, but no harm done. Emmanuel is too hard on himself.

"No one will see with icing on them," I reply, clasping his shoulder warmly. "We open in fifteen."

"I'll get everything out to Renee," Emmanuel says. "After I frost these fuckers."

The back door swings open and my sister walks in, a cloud of perfume accompanying her. I wrinkle my nose at the sickly-sweet scent.

When she sees me, she grimaces. "Sorry I'm late." Candy is nearly always late, and, on occasion, doesn't bother to come in at all. "Traffic was hell." The corner of her lip twitches at her own joke. She lives above Ebb and Flow in a loft apartment.

"Yeah, I'm sure." I roll my eyes. Candy gives me a one-armed hug, kissing my temple. "How are you doing?" she asks quietly.

"I'd be better if my ex wasn't living above my cafe," I grumble. It's as though I can feel him up there. From his vantage point above, is he omniscient like a god? Is every shiver down my spine because we've crossed paths?

"What could I say? 'No, you can't stay here, Geoff. Be homeless.'"

"*Yes*," I deadpan.

"He's been asking about you," Candy says slowly. She searches my face as if trying to glean whether I'd be receptive to the information. *I'm not,* but she pushes onward anyway. "I think he's having a change of heart."

"I'm not," I snap, brushing past her to enter my office. She's shaken me, and I don't want her to see. It will inevitably get back to Geoff. After all, Candy's allegiance is tenuous at best. She doesn't think our argument was worth breaking up over.

The morning rush begins as usual. Eddie comes in for his coffee and bagel, coyly sliding the hardcover James Patterson book across the counter as though we are engaging in a drug deal. All of the faces in the cafe are familiar. I don't know them all by name, but we have all certainly bumped elbows in the grocery store or passed one another on the street.

Renee and I work in tandem. When she makes drinks, I take orders, and vice versa.

"Heads up," Renee whispers, her voice barely audible over the hiss of the milk steamer.

As I pour foamed milk into a dark pool of espresso, I look up and into the eyes of Geoff, my ex-boyfriend. My stomach drops at his easy smile, the notch in his canine tooth from when he fell off a curb as a kid. I haven't seen him since he moved out of my bungalow a few weeks ago when his shoulders slumped under his heavy bags.

He looks good. His hair, a burnished copper, is windswept. He's wearing one of my t-shirts. He must have taken it by accident. Or maybe he wanted it because it smelt like me.

"Hunt," he says by way of greeting. "Are you going to take my order?" He gestures at the unmanned register, raising his eyebrows. I look to Renee, hoping she is free to do it instead, but she's elbow-deep in the pastry case, searching for the perfect baked brie pastry for Mr. Bartlett, the crotchety old postmaster. Or perhaps, Candy…but she's making frappes for a group of giggling tweens.

Shit.

I step over to the register, waking it with a keypress. "What can I get you?" I manage. It's hard to talk when a lump of emotion is lodged in my throat. Though it had been my decision to break up, it still hurts all the same.

"A coffee with milk," he replies. "You know how I like it." There's a suggestion there, but I ignore it. I pour coffee from the carafe and add milk until the liquid turns beige, then wordlessly set the lidded cup on the countertop, not wanting our hands to touch. I don't think I can stomach it.

"How much?" he prompts.

"$2.50."

He coolly pulls three-dollar bills from his wallet, then hands them to me. I fish two quarters out of the register and place them in his palm. The pad of his finger brushes against my wrist. *Was that on purpose?* "Thanks," he says as he grabs his coffee, blowing on the thin wisp of steam trickling from the spout. I miss those lips; they are so soft and pink like sakura flowers. "You look good," he remarks.

"I—"

"Hey, man," rumbles a deep voice from behind Geoff. "Some of us are waiting to order."

Startled, Geoff steps aside, letting the next customer approach the register. I've never seen him before. He is tall and thick, his wavy hair long enough to barely touch his shoulders. He wears a long-sleeved dress shirt, the top three buttons undone, and the sleeves rolled up his elbows. It's hot and humid out. I can feel the oppressive thickness each time the door opens. *He must be sweltering.* "Can I get two iced coffees?" the man asks. "One with a bit of soy milk."

"Sure thing," I reply, avoiding Geoff's gaze. As I move to the fridge to retrieve the soy milk, Geoff shadows me on the other side of the counter. "Can we talk?" he asks.

"Later," I snap. "I have customers."

"I know. I was just thinking about what you said, and—" What I said was that I wanted *more*. He, clearly, wanted less.

"*Later*," I repeat, slamming the fridge shut. I don't know if I even want to hear how that sentence ends. Even if it's *'you were right, Hunter'*.

Geoff presses his lips together, and mumbles something incomprehensible before heading toward a table in the back corner of the cafe.

I turn my attention back to my customer. "I'm sorry about that," I mumble. "I'm usually not this unprofessional."

"It's okay," he says kindly. "I'm usually not this sweaty." He raises his arms just enough for me to see the dark, wet patches under his arms. "I forgot how humid it is on the East Coast."

I quickly finish preparing his order and place it on the countertop. The cups are wet with condensation, so I dry my hands on the front of my jeans. "Oh, are you visiting someone?"

Now that Geoff is no longer within arm's length, forcing me to look inward, I am suddenly very aware of how attractive the stranger is. He is Geoff's antithesis: rugged, muscular, and intense. His eyes bore into me, and my cheeks grow hot. I hope that I'm not blushing. I hope *Geoff* doesn't see me blushing.

"I'm staying with my grandmother," the man says. He pulls out a debit card and hands it to me. For a second, I stare at it stupidly. Then, I remember I haven't actually completed his transaction. *Hunter, get it together*, I admonish myself. I run the card and try to get a peek at the name written in block letters on the front. *AN—something*.

"What's her name? I might know her." I stare at the screen until the card processes, then hand it back. His thumb briefly touches mine. His skin is calloused and warm. The firmness of it startles me, like I hadn't expected him to be tangible.

"Ama Chilton," he replies, taking a sip of his iced coffee, the one with soy milk.

I know the name. She lives at the opposite end of Bird's Nest, the same street I live on. While I'm near the dunes, her bungalow is closer to the wave breakers, a pile of concrete tetrapods placed haphazardly along the shoreline. They remind me of a game of jacks, the pieces thrown by gargantuan titans. I've seen Ama walking down the lane, her gait more of a stumble than a stride. A waifish woman that looks as though she'll blow away if the wind comes off the sea at just the right angle. *I can't believe she's related to this oak tree of a man.*

"I've seen her around," I say. "We live on the same street."

"Oh yeah?" He grins.

A long-haired woman appears beside him, standing so close they bump shoulders. Her arms are laden with shopping bags from Marnie's, the local clothing boutique. Her sunglasses are large and reflective; my own face, slightly distorted, looks back at me. Her shirt, ostensibly from Marnie's, still has the tag on it, tucked into her armpit. It's an overly large men's button down, paired with cutoff jeans.

She pushes her sunglasses up onto her head to reveal large, dark eyes and the absence of eyebrows. *Does she shave them off?*

"I'm done," she announces. The man hands her the other iced coffee without looking at her. "Oh, thanks, Angus!" she squeals, taking a sip.

Angus.

Angus is still looking at me, his lips pursed around his straw. After a long moment of silence, he licks his lips, the tip of his tongue swiping coffee off his lower lip. "I guess I'll see you around then," he says, "since you live so close." He holds out his hand to shake. "I'm Angus," he says.

I take the proffered hand. His grip is firm. "It's nice to meet you," I reply, relieved that my voice doesn't tremble. *Is he interested in me?* I'm certainly interested in him.

The woman gives me a little wave. "I'm Leigh," she chirps. "This cafe is so cute!"

"Thanks," I reply as heat creeps up my neck and settles in my cheeks. I had inherited the building from my parents. Before, it had been a shop selling chotskies to the tourists swarming the beaches every summer. My mom, an amateur artist, airbrushed names in elaborate cursive over neon images of palm trees, dolphins, and butterflies. Despite vigorous scrubbing and a fresh coat of lacquer, there are still smudges of paint on this very countertop.

Leigh points at the shelves of ceramic mugs behind me. "Are those handmade? They're *darling*."

Geoff made them. I picture him on the back deck of our bungalow, his body hunched over his pottery wheel and his hands wet with clay. He always wears the same linen pants when he works, the fabric flecked with flyaway kaolin clay and drips of acrylic paint. He wears them so often that the waistband is worn, nearly falling off his narrow hips when he rises from the wheel. "Yeah," I tell her. "They're made by a local artist."

"This town is so cute," Leigh gushes. "It's not like Po—"

Angus coughs.

"—I mean, it's not like anywhere I've ever been." She flicks her long hair over her shoulder. "I'm a city girl."

"Well, welcome," I say brightly.

"Let's head home," Angus tells his companion, his voice pointed. Before they go, he reaches across the counter and tilts my name badge to read it. His finger brushes against my chest. "I'll see you around, *Hunter.*"

After they leave, I absently wipe the counters with a damp cloth. *Was Angus flirting?* He is definitely attractive, and I can't help but imagine what running my fingers through his long hair would feel like. A butterfly takes wing in my stomach, then shrivels to dust when Geoff catches my eye. We haven't been broken up for more than a month, and I'm already ogling a handsome stranger.

I'm an asshole.

CHAPTER THREE
(ANGUS)

———— ◁◆▷ ————

Walking through Wharton is surreal, like remembering a dream: a blur of shape and color with moments of clarity.

I find Marnie's, the clothing boutique, without much trouble, though I remember it as Sandbar Thrift. When I wander down Main Street, I find many of my old haunts: the arcade, Dottie's Diner nestled beneath the eaves of the motel, and an ice cream shop called Swirly's touting a "World Famous Chocolate-Dipped Cone." But all of the buildings look smaller now, less thrilling. Ten-year-old Angus had found this place extraordinary, an interlude from school and the unyielding cold of Maine.

Ama never seemed tired of me, unlike my workaholic parents.

When I was a child, Ebb and Flow was a t-shirt shop. The owners kept the doors propped open, the air conditioning a welcome respite from the humidity. My mother bought me a shirt there once: a beachy sunset emblazoned with my name. Now, walking into the shop is a wholly different experience. There are no longer racks upon racks of shirts and bathing suits, but cafe tables adorned with small succulent plants and little cards chronicling the week's events: poetry readings, open mics, and the like.

Early 2000s alternative rock has replaced The Beach Boys discography while the woman behind the counter — sunburnt arms and tired eyes — has been replaced by *him*.

I think about the barista as Leigh and I walk down the boardwalk. *Hunter.* He couldn't stop smiling at me, though he made every effort not to. He even avoided my eyes, biting at his lip with his herbivore teeth, like the scared rabbits I've occasionally stalked in Oregon: flighty, fidgety, with wide, darting eyes.

"This coffee is so good," Leigh gushes, nearly trotting to keep up with my long stride. She's been almost manic since we arrived in Wharton, eager to overcompensate for the behavior of her surlier twin. "I hope these clothes fit everyone," she muses.

"I'm sure it'll be fine," I assure her, though I'm not really listening. I'm troubled. I've commingled with hundreds of humans in my lifetime, and I've had a handful of genuine friends. But I rail against our most primal instincts, despite the tug in my stomach whenever I stand too close.

I wish I could blame it on our recent hurried excursion across the Shenandoah Mountains when we only stopped to sleep or hunt the occasional hare. We slept curled around one another; noses tucked under tails. Wolfish. I dreamt of hunting, killing, and eating.

I would never tell a soul; but sometimes, I dreamt that I was in the car with Ronnie, too.

I shouldn't be thinking about the barista, I admonish myself. But he's beautiful, *isn't he?*

The chilled coffee sloshes as I clutch my half-empty cup, remembering the way he poured the dark roast over ice while I stared at the knob of his wrist.

He's so fragile. I wanted to grip his wrist, run the pad of my thumb along the tendons there, and press my nose against him, inhaling his heady scent and dragging my tongue across his paper-thin skin. Even in the cafe, my senses inundated with the aroma of freshly ground coffee beans, I still managed to catch a whiff of him. He smelled faintly like almond soap. It's easy to imagine Hunter in the shower, scrubbing the back of his neck with a sudsy loofah.

Stop it, I admonish myself.

As Leigh and I stroll down Bird's Nest, I examine the row of bungalows. *Which one is his?* They're all identical, save for the color of the facades and the bits and bobs on the porch. Maybe his is the one with the retro, powder blue 7-speed leaning against the railing, its front wheel akimbo. Or perhaps it's the one with the weathered Adirondack chair, a paperback with a cracked spine balanced on the armrest.

Soon, Ama's bungalow comes into view, and I give up my game.

In the daylight, her home looks more dilapidated than I thought. It's as though her house was overtaken by a tsunami, leaving behind random debris in the yard and swaths of fauna on the flat roof. I toe aside a felled yard flamingo, its curved neck infringing on the walking path. *I need to clean this place up later.* Clearly, it's all too much for Ama. She'll never admit it, but it's apparent she is struggling living alone. Her fridge is bare, and laundry is piled atop the washer into a treacherous peak.

James sits on the uneven porch steps, smoking a cigarette. He's shirtless, and the borrowed dress slacks are far too short, revealing his naked ankles. The wisps of silver at his temples look fiery in the sunlight. He's been there for a while, his chest already sun-kissed, taking on a burnished, auriferous quality.

He says nothing as we approach, his eyes half-lidded.

"Hey," Leigh says, ruffling his hair. He growls, swatting at her none-too-gently. She deftly side-steps him, dropping a shopping bag into his lap. "I bought you a present," she admonishes him. "Be nice." She heads inside, the screen door squealing on its hinges.

James grunts, opening the bag with the cigarette dangling between his lips. I sink down on the porch step beside him, the lopsidedness causing our hips to press together. Despite my unyielding anger, I find myself sinking into his warmth until our shoulders touch, too. We fit together, his sharp edges tucking into my softer corners like a sheathed knife.

I hate him, but he feels like home.

"Please tell me this town is more exciting than this fucking house," James grunts.

I shrug, and our left and right shoulders rise in tandem. "It's how I remember it. Nicer shops, though." I take a sip of my iced coffee. "Less tourists, though I guess the season is over, isn't it?" I think of the fierce cold we endured while running through the mountains mere days ago. The cold hasn't quite reached this sleepy beach town, but the clouds are a constant gray, thick with rain that never comes.

James peers at the coffee cup's logo, a mug with an ocean wave cresting the rim. "Ebb and Flow," he reads. "Is everything here so twee and aggressively beachy?"

"I like it," I say, feeling defensive. Wharton isn't as cultured as James is accustomed to, but it's our home. *At least temporarily.* James wouldn't be here if he hadn't killed the Nedry boy. This is his punishment. At least it's not jail.

Or *worse*, his grotesque wolf head impaled on a pike, his eyes wide and unseeing.

"Angus sure liked the handsome barista behind the counter," Leigh remarks, returning to the porch. Luka trails behind her, having changed into a pair of well-fitted jeans and a horizontally striped tee that she picked up at the boutique.

Luka idly sips the watery dregs of Leigh's leftover coffee. Thick bags cause his eyes to droop, like an exhausted hound dog.

I startle. Leigh's expression is unreadable. While her voice is teasing, I wonder if her motives are less than good-natured. Her allegiance is, at best, tenuous. James is her brother, after all.

Smoke trickles out of James' nose as he turns to survey me. "Oh yeah?" he murmurs, raising his thick eyebrows, the corner of his lip twitching. *A smile, or a grimace?*

I shrug. "He was nice," I reply, waving away the smoke. "I was being kind."

"You were nearly salivating." Leigh laughs. "I don't blame you. He was gorgeous."

"I wasn't salivating," I counter, rising from the porch steps, absently brushing the dust from the back of my pants. "This is ridiculous. Let's clean up and earn our keep around here."

♦ ♦ ♦

Ama's shower is a small, claustrophobic cubicle. The water shoots from the nozzle in coughing spurts and smells faintly metallic. I wash with a thinning bar of Dial soap and Pantene shampoo meant for gray hair. Afterward, I pad, dripping down the hall to the tiny guest bedroom, eager to dress and go to bed.

My body is sore. The yard work took hours. Inside, we barely made a dent. Sweating under the single overhead fan, we organized Ama's possessions into three piles: keep, throw away, and items that should be thrown away but Ama insists on keeping regardless. "I might need that," she chirped as Luka unraveled a long CVS receipt dated March 2017.

The guest room is occupied. Luka and Leigh sleep in the double bed, the latter softly snoring. There's no room for me. I dry off in the doorway and find the satchel of underwear Leigh had purchased for me ("Plain black," she'd said. "I know a pattern wouldn't suit you"). *I guess I'll just sleep in the living room on the pull-out sofa.* I'd slept on it—or rather, laid on it— the night before, thanks to an errant spring that dug into my back the entire night.

Feeling around the living room furniture by touch alone, I find the couch is already taken.

James lays on his stomach, starfished on the thin mattress. He's naked, save for a pair of polka-dotted boxers ("You can pull these off, Jay," Leigh laughed, handing him the satchel with waggling eyebrows). In his sleep, he shrugged off the blanket, and now, it's tangled around his legs. I have to untangle it to slip into bed too. His muscles involuntarily flex under my touch, and he murmurs in his sleep.

I am unprepared for the wave of contented familiarity that overtakes me when I slide into bed beside him. *I miss this—him.*

For just a moment, my anger fades. I tuck my chin into the curve of his shoulder, wrapping an arm around his thick waist. I'll only let myself do this for a moment. Just one more second. *James and I are completely over.*

"Mm," James mumbles, and I jerk away as if caught with my hand in the cookie jar. I roll away, pulling the blanket over my shoulders. For a long while, I listen to his even breathing and am nearly lulled to sleep myself.

"A human, Angus?" he suddenly asks, his voice startling me back into wakefulness.

"What?" I roll over, and we are suddenly nose-to-nose. His breath smells like stale tobacco and spearmint toothpaste. His eyes are black holes.

"You weren't really flirting with a human, were you?" he asks.

"Excuse me?" I prop myself onto my elbow, peering down at him. The only light comes from the porchlight outside. Shadows mask his face, making it impossible to read his expression.

"I just wanted to ensure the sea air hasn't fucked with your brain." His teeth glint as he smirks. His tone is dangerous, rattled. Clearly, his sister's innocent observation had hurt his feelings. I didn't quite believe he had any feelings left—for me, or for anything else. Any day now, I half expect him to just disappear without a single word. *I don't want it,* he'd said. *I don't want your shitty little pack.*

"What are you getting at?"

"I'm just saying...don't make a stupid mistake," he replies.

I guffaw. James has some *nerve.*

The pack will forever be haunted by what he did, dogged across the country by the threat of arrest or worse, *death.* Nedry's blood is on all of our hands—and paws.

"Go to sleep, Jay," I tell him, laughing. I rise, not willing to engage in this conversation any longer. He is making a mountain out of a molehill. Hunter is beautiful, but I'm not looking for a relationship, not even a one-night stand. I step out onto the front porch, the humidity striking my face like a cough. Cicadas trill, thousands of voices creating a torrent of sound. I settle on the porch in my underwear, resting my elbows on my knees. "Don't make a stupid mistake," I scoff, repeating James' words as my voice is drowned out by the bugs' incessant chirruping.

Chapter Three (angus)

It's midday, and I stroll down Main Street, searching for the grocery store. I'm not sure where the local market is, allowing Ama's vague directions and my own childhood memories to lead the way. I pause on the corner of Main and Bonnet Drive, trying to get my bearings. The thoroughfare is crowded today, but I'm head and shoulders over most of the denizens in Wharton.

I turn in a slow circle, drawing my lips into a thin line.

"Are you lost?"

Startled, I twirl and find myself ensnared in Hunter's sea-green eyes. He's dressed much the same as yesterday: jeans and a faded t-shirt, minus the apron and nametag. His cheeks redden as I stare at him, stupefied. I wasn't expecting to see him here. Though, I admit...I was considering stopping by Ebb and Flow before returning to Ama's. I nearly convinced myself it was just for another iced coffee. It *was* delicious.

"I thought there was a grocery store around here. But ten-year-old me was probably too busy staring at beefcakes in speedos to recall *where* it is." I laugh.

Hunter's blush deepens. "You're close. It's only a block that way." He gestures down Bonnet Drive.

The smell of him fills my nostrils, and I find myself stepping closer. It seems to startle him. His body spasms, and I imagine his muscles flooding with adrenaline. Perhaps he does realize what I am, in some deep, primeval part of himself. *Run away, little one. Quickly!*

"Thank you," I reply. *He probably doesn't remember me*. I turn to walk down Bonnet, but his fingertips touch my elbow.

"You're Angus, right?" he asks. He's tentative, his eyes flitting from my face, to the street, to his own scuffed shoes. He must see hundreds of customers a day, but for some reason…he remembers *me*.

Heat pools in my groin. I think of my fantasy, the image of him soaping his neck with a loofah, water pouring over his thin shoulders. I imagine taking the sponge from his hand, sliding it down the curvature of his spine. *Stop it,* I reprimand myself.

"Yeah," I reply. "I remember you too, Hunter." I like saying his name: an inhale, a tap of the tongue against the teeth, and a growl. *Hunter.* "It's nice to see you again." I hold out my hand to shake, and he takes it. An excuse to touch.

"Yeah," Hunter says softly. "I need to get back to the cafe, but don't be a stranger, okay?" He releases my hand and nearly speed-walks past me, crossing the crosswalk to continue down Main Street. I watch him go. He ducks his head, rubbing his palm along the back of his neck. That neck I've imagined suds trickling down, my lips following suit. *I might like to bite him, just above where the trapezius meets the scapula. I imagine the salt of his sweat on my tongue.*

Stop.

He glances back and gives me a small wave, nearly colliding with a woman walking a small dog. I chuckle as he untangles himself from the dog's lead, apologizing profusely.

He's cute.

CHAPTER FOUR
(HUNTER)

———⊲◆⊳———

On Sunday, Ebb and Flow is quiet. Our usual patrons are attending church services or completing the chores they've been putting off all week. Renee is hungover, and sits at one of the cafe tables, her chin resting heavily on her palm. She winces each time the door opens, sliding off the stool with an exaggerated bleat. I ignore her, focusing on the piles of receipts and pages of scrawled notes before me.

Like Renee's Sunday morning hangover, this is my ritual.

The door opens, and Renee peels herself off the tabletop, stepping behind the counter. Two people approach the counter, one I recognize: the dark-haired woman who had come in with Angus the other day. *I can't remember her name.* The other is a slender black man, dreads piled atop his head in a thick Gordian knot. I want to ask the woman about Angus. *Is he available?*

I shouldn't ask. Geoff has only just moved out. There are still indentations in the carpet from where his guitar used to stand. He still texts asking for *this* or *that* he had left behind. Rebounds never last, *right?* But still, Angus' smile makes my face hot. I can't help but to imagine what his hands—rough-hewn, with fingers that seem impossibly long—would feel like on my hips, my spine, fisting my hair.

Drinks in hand, the woman and man sit at a table nearby, chatting. Renee disappears into the back of the shop, presumably to vomit or guzzle that violently blue Gatorade she favors. I try to return to my pile of papers, tapping the button on my calculator so that it resets to zero. But then the woman notices me.

"You own this place, right?" she asks, turning in her seat to survey me. She crosses her long legs, the skin impossibly unblemished: no bruises, no white scars from falling off a bicycle as a kid. *Nothing.* It's like she's been airbrushed.

"That's me," I reply.

"I'm Leigh," she says. "This is Luka." Luka smiles tightly at me, his hands encircling the ceramic mug before him, his nails bitten to the quick.

"I remember you," I tell her. "I'm Hunter. Hunter Bailey."

"Our friend Angus has been raving about this place," Leigh says. "I didn't know he was such a caffeine addict. But maybe—" Her eyes flick up and down my body, "—maybe he's more interested in the handsome barista than the menu." *Has Angus been talking about me?* He stops by every few days for his signature drink (iced coffee, soy milk) and lingers at the counter to chat with me.

He's easy to talk to, easy to laugh with.

He makes excuses to *touch* me.

Once, we ran into one another in the vestibule leading to the bathrooms and he touched my waist to get by. *It* may have been my imagination, but I swear he held on for a moment too long. Since then, I have fostered a fantasy where he leads me into the bathroom and kisses me behind the locked door, his hands trailing down my sides, his fingers hooking my belt loops, his hardening—*stop it, Hunter!*

"Oh," I say, my voice even. Inside though, my heart flutters. I try very hard not to think of Geoff, or the texts I've left on read.

[Geoff: I miss you.]
[Geoff: Can we please talk?]
[Geoff: I really do love you, you know.]

I repeatedly tap my pen on the tabletop, unsure what to do with my hands.

Leigh rests her chin on her palm, surveying me. "Are you married?"

"I don't want to get married," Geoff says in exasperation, slamming our bedroom door. "How many times must I say it?" I hear him pulling blankets from the linen closet and tossing them onto the living room couch, building himself a nest in which to sleep.

Chagrined, I open the door, stepping into the hall. "Come back to bed," I plead. "I'm sorry."

"I'm tired of the guilt trip." Geoff's eyes meet mine; he has turned on the lamp, and the warm glow makes him appear particularly pale. His hair is a wildfire, interlaced with rivulets of liquid gold. "I don't know why this *can't be enough."*

I want this to be enough, too. But it's not.

He continues, *"I won't be tied to someone. I love you, but I won't be like my mother, unable to leave my fucking dad."*

Geoff's father lives in a six by eight cell at Keen Mountain Correctional. Geoff visits him every few months, and always returns sullen and introspective.

"I don't know how he lives like that," he often muses afterward. "It's awful."

When Geoff gets drunk, he describes it to me: tall walls, the squawk of radios and the jangle of keys, the thick plexiglass that separates himself from his father. Even the god-awful wails when his father presses his forehead against the glass partition separating them, sobbing, I'm sorry, I'm sorry, I'm so, so sorry.

"He looks like a stranger," Geoff whispers between shots of Jameson. "It's like he ages ten years every time I visit."

When he visits his mother, he returns with red-rimmed eyes. She's little more than a memory now. He likes to clean up her tombstone and put fresh flowers in the vase. He reads her favorite quote by Cormac McCarthy over and over, which is etched into the facade of her tombstone: "Keep a little fire burning; however small, however hidden."

Any mention of his parents is like a slap. Does he see something—my character, my mannerisms, my desires—that reminds him of his father? "Do you think that little of me?" I ask.

"No. I don't know. But can't we just fucking sleep?"

"I'm not married," I tell Leigh. "I'm single, actually."

"Do you know of any good bars?" Leigh asks. "We've only been in town for a few weeks. Luka and

I like to have fun." The implication is that Angus isn't fun, or at least, has a different idea as to what constitutes fun.

"Sure," I reply. "I like the barcade off of Jefferson Ave—Freddie's.

"That sounds cool," Luka says, excited.

"Why don't you come with us?" Leigh suggests, her eyes scanning the nearly empty cafe. The only patron is a college student wearing a Wharton Community College sweatshirt, typing furiously on her computer. "It doesn't seem very busy here."

Normally, I wouldn't leave the cafe, even working through the dissolution of my relationship, excusing myself to the back office to cry between patrons. But it's a slow day. The thought of hanging out with Angus' friends sounds exciting. "Sure. I'd like that."

Before we head out, I bus the table Leigh and Luka had occupied. Leigh's latte is untouched, the swirl of foam unbroken.

♦ ♦ ♦

Freddie's is nearly empty. We are several hours early for happy hour.

Luka bounds into the arcade, fingering the joysticks and tapping buttons while the screens flash INSERT COIN, INSERT COIN, INSERT COIN. "They have the old school Ninja Turtles!" he whoops. "Turtles in time!"

Leigh rolls her eyes, making a beeline toward the bar. "Sometimes I forget he's only nineteen," she says.

"How did you meet?" I ask. I had assumed they were adopted siblings. They seem inordinately close, more so than two friends should feasibly be. Leigh and Luka spent the entire walk from Ebb and Flow to Freddie's arm-in-arm, communicating in half-sentences. They may as well have been speaking another language. It was all in-jokes and exaggerated facial expressions.

"He's a family friend," she replies, resting her elbows on the bar top.

She's wearing an oversized t-shirt as a dress that inches up her thighs as she beckons for the bartender. He's engrossed in conversation with another patron, but he pulls himself away when he sees the beautiful woman vying for his attention. And Leigh is obviously gorgeous, tall and sylphlike.

"Can I get vodka on the rocks and a Natty Ice?" she asks when the bartender approaches. Then, she turns to me. "What's your poison?"

"A rum and coke for me," I say, easing onto a stool, shaking the tension from my shoulders. Being here feels surreal. I never go out for drinks—certainly not before noon. Leaving Ebb and Flow in Renee's hands feels all the more bizarre. She's more than capable, but the cafe is such an integral part of my identity. But there's a certain *je ne sais quoi* about Angus' friends. They are so inviting, so free-spirited, so…*otherworldly* that I find myself wanting to delve deeply into their friend group, trace the through lines and find out *which strands lead to Angus*.

When my drink arrives, I take a sip. The bartender was *very* generous with the rum, and the sugar lingers on the tip of my tongue long after I've swallowed. "How are you liking Wharton?"

Before answering, Leigh asks the bartender for eight quarters, handing him two crisp bills in return. "It's nice," she says. "Sleepy, for a beach town."

"You should see it in the summertime," I say as she leads the way toward the arcade. The coins jingle in her fist as she hands me her vodka to hold.

It takes several minutes to find Luka. He stands before the *Time Crisis 4* cabinet, pretending to shoot the light gun.

"I got you quarters," Leigh tells him, "and a beer."

"Leigh, he's underage," I whisper. "We'll get into trouble."

"We won't get into trouble," Leigh replies. "Luka looks *at least* twenty-five."

Luka takes a swig of his beer. "C'mon Hunter, play this game with me." Leigh takes her drink and mine from my hands, tilting her chin toward the cabinet as if to say, *go on*. I relent and take the second joystick. As we play, I find myself laughing and joking around. Luka and I elbow each other as we move from cabinet to cabinet, talking trash.

"You aren't even old enough to know this game," I snort as we play *Polybius* on a nondescript cabinet, the paint peeling. I smash the brightly colored buttons with my palm.

"Okay, *grandpa*," Luka replies. His beer sweats atop the cabinet, the condensation pooling.

The ice rattles in Leigh's glass as she drinks the dregs of her second vodka. "I can see what Angus sees in you," Leigh says.

"How so?" I ask, before I can even process the thought that he *sees* something—anything—in me.

"You're the opposite of my brother," she says. Her voice is cool though she doesn't seem particularly accusatory. *Was Angus seeing her brother?* Or rather, *is* he? "Not entirely different," she amends. "Just in every way that counts." My expression must have betrayed me because she laughs. "Don't worry. Their *thing* is over."

"Oh," I reply uneasily. If Leigh is here, surely her brother is, too. I may have served him coffee or passed him on the pier. "Where's your brother now?"

Leigh shrugs. "Around." Luka coughs, bending over the machine and slapping the buttons with a particular frenetic energy, his nose mere inches from the screen. Leigh leans against a *Mrs. Pac-Man* machine. Her eyes are the color of dark chocolate and betray nothing, her facade impassive. "You like Angus, right?"

Lie to her. Talking to her about this feels *dangerous*. But she's disarmed me with her kindness and several rum and cokes. "Yeah," I say slowly. "He's nice."

Leigh reaches toward me, and I flinch. But she merely brushes a stray wisp of hair from my forehead, tucking it behind my ear. A strange gesture reserved for a family member or a lifelong friend.

"Come on," she cajoles. "Don't be shy. I'll never tell."

My head swims. The alcohol sinks its teeth into my arm, dragging me down into blurriness and improvidence. And Leigh seems so *nice*. I hate to admit it, but I have very few genuine friends. The ones I'd shared with Geoff chose him over me. I don't know if it was intentional, but it cut like a knife. It's hard to contend with the notion that I might be unlikeable. And it doesn't help that I'm also inaccessible; I work every day, all day long. *I'm lonely.*

"I think he's handsome. I enjoy our conversations when he comes in. My phone vibrates in my pocket, and I fish it out, looking at the screen.

[Renee: Time for lunch. Close up?]

I am shocked by the time. I've been hanging out with Leigh and Luka for well over an hour. I type a response:

[Hunter: I'll be back in five.]

"I have to go," I tell my new friends.

"We'll walk you back," Leigh offers. "We should be heading home, too."

After the dark bar, the sunlight makes me squint. Black motes swim before my eyes. Instantly, a sheen of sweat prickles on my brow. "Y'know, we're having a little birthday party for Angus' granny," Leigh continues. "She's turning ninety-five, can you imagine? We are having a bonfire on the beach tonight to celebrate. How about you come?" She glances at her companion. "Doesn't that sound like *such* a good idea?"

"Sure," Luka manages. "Yeah." I look at him curiously, but his face is impassive. "Maybe," he coughs, "we could order some of those cookies from the cafe, too. The ones in the case."

"I would love to come," I say. "But I don't want to intrude."

"Nonsense," Leigh says with a chuckle. "We'd love to have you. Otherwise, it's just us and Ama's

45

friends from her knitting circle. The bonfire starts at dusk behind the dunes. Come whenever."

When I step inside the cool cafe, Leigh gives me a little wave from the other side of the frosted glass. It warps her features, making her look as though she's exploded into hundreds of pieces.

Wharton at sunset is an entirely different animal from early morning. It is loud, thick with the voices of out-of-towners, reveling on the beach and poolside. Even now, in the off-season, there are still quite a few milling outside the Wharton Great Inn.

I stop at home after the cafe, eager to shower before heading to the beach. My cat, Ghost, meows at me from atop the couch, his eyes two narrow, sleepy slits. I toss a scoop of kibble into his bowl before heading into the bathroom to shower.

The setting sun shooting through the skylight turns the bathroom pink. I undress and step into the shower cubicle. My thoughts shift to Angus, about the way the firelight will paint his cheeks and the slope of his forehead. I think of pulling him just beyond the circle of the fire's glow, kissing him on the mouth. As I imagine him laying me down on the dunes, his kisses trailing down my neck, I stroke my hardening cock. *God. I wonder what sort of lover he is. Is he gentle? Or will he rip at my clothes with wild abandon, his teeth branding my skin?* I don't know which I hope for.

I rest my palm against the cool tile, leaning into the ministrations of my free hand, running the pad of my thumb over the sensitive slit at the head of my cock, my balls tightening deliciously. As I imagine kneeling in the sand, the sea grass tickling my thighs, Angus' cock sliding wetly against my soft palate, I cum.

After drying off, I pad into my bedroom, dressing in jeans and a faded Metric band tee. I don't want to look like I'm trying too hard, or that I expect this to be a date. I run my hands through my wet hair; it will air dry on the way.

My phone chimes. It's Geoff.

[Geoff: Can we meet tonight?]

I sigh. I wish he would stop. He made his choice. He was the one who didn't want to get married. He was the one who said he was stagnating, that playing house wasn't what he imagined for himself.

Agitated, I tap out a quick response.

[Hunter: I have a date.]

He doesn't respond.

◆ ◆ ◆

It takes a lot of confused meandering to find the bonfire, tucked between two steep dunes, the sparks barely visible from the beach proper. I try to walk down the incline, but I lose my balance, sliding and sprinting down its length to avoid falling on my ass. I straighten my clothes, grateful that my blush of embarrassment can be explained away. The heat from the blaze is already extreme and sweat seeps out of my pores at an alarming rate. A terrifying thought bubbles up, popping on the surface of my consciousness—*you blew it*. Between my inelegant arrival and my heavy perspiration, Angus likely won't give me the time of day.

Leigh trots across the thick sand. "You made it!" She nearly bounces on her toes like an excited puppy as she deftly takes the box of cookies from my hand and replaces it with a chilly beer.

She leads me fireside. The fire roars like an animal, a freight train, a roaring dinosaur that's nearly overwhelming in its ferocity.

"You remember Luka," Leigh says, gesturing to the man sitting in the sand. Luka shoots me a tight smile and inclines his chin.

Then, she propels me toward another man who I have never seen before. His hair is a striking salt-and-pepper, his eyebrows thick and jet black. He has the same high cheekbones as Leigh. In fact, they look uncannily similar, though this man is muscular and outweighs her by at least a hundred pounds.

"This is my brother James," she says. "I told you about him."

She had, but she didn't say that he's preternaturally gorgeous. Unlike myself, he's sinewy, broad and heavily tattooed with a bright red Hannya mask adorning his throat. He is like a bird of paradise, albeit a terrifying one.

"So," James says with a hollow grin. "This is the famous Hunter." His unblinking eyes bore into mine, dark and empty, akin to the eyes of a Great White shark. He makes me feel uneasy.

You're just projecting. Surely, he isn't forcing my heart to hammer *danger, danger, danger.* Still, I've never met someone who's made me feel this uncomfortable before.

"Nice to meet you," I say, my mouth dry. I take a swig of my beer.

"I can see why Angus likes you," James says coolly. "You're like an innocent baby bunny waiting for his mama."

At the mention of his name, I look for Angus, but he isn't at the bonfire. Nor is Ama Chilton and her supposed knitting circle. "Where—" I begin.

James claps a hand on my shoulder, giving me a shake. "Tell us a little about yourself, Hunter. You married?"

Luka rises from the sand, ungainly. "Jay." His voice is sharp, the edge serrated. I've only heard him speak jubilantly with the zealousness of someone very young. "Stop."

James glances at Luka without taking his hand off me. "Everything is fine," he tells the younger man. "Chill." His fingers tighten around my scapula.

Luka sighs, hanging his head. "This isn't cool, man." But he steps back, reaching into the cooler for a beer. "Not cool at all." The bottle opens with a *hiss,* and he tips it back, swallowing vigorously. It's like he's trying to drown himself.

I know the feeling.

"You married?" James repeats, looking at me intently.

"No," I reply. "I'm not."

"Angus didn't tell you he was married, did he?"

Despite the fire's heat, a chill envelopes me like I've been plunged into ice water. *Married?* James stands so close that I have to put my palms on his chest to keep from tumbling backward. The cloying scent of wood smoke fills my nostrils.

"Oh," I stammer. I must sound childish, incapable of forming a complete sentence. *This feels like an ambush.* I look for Leigh or Luka for help, but they're midway up the dune, carrying a cooler between them. Neither look back.

Bits and bobs of their conversation reaches my ears, carried by the sea wind. *He... stop...die!* Die?

"Were you planning to fuck my husband?" James asks. His face is impassive. He may as well be asking something totally banal. *How's the weather?*

Only James and I remain in the heated circle. I feel dizzy. Every time James inhales, it's as though he's stealing all the oxygen in the air. "I didn't..." James' face seems to elongate, his short beard trailing up his cheeks. *Yes. I'm* definitely *having a panic attack;* my vision swims.

I step back, mumbling apologies. "I didn't know, I'm sorry, I'm gonna go h—"

"No," he whispers. His palm encircles the back of my neck, keeping me close. "I don't think so." His breath is hot. As hot as the fire over his shoulder. Hotter, even. His voice, already deep, is suddenly throaty and the bass of it rumbles in my chest. It's as though I'm standing too close to a speaker at a concert. "Gus would never be able to resist you. But he's mine."

He squeezes, and it feels as though he's cutting me with something pronged and incredibly sharp. The pain is immeasurable. *Where had he been hiding a weapon?* I swing wildly, bottle in hand, but I don't make contact. He grasps the bottle with his free hand, tossing it over his shoulder.

His face isn't a face anymore. It's as though I blinked, and he became something else entirely. *A wolf!* Or rather, a grotesque amalgamation of wolf and man. The wolf curls his lips from his jaws, his myriad teeth sharp and dripping with thick drool. He drags his long, pink tongue along his incisors and long canines. *My...what big fucking teeth you have.* He lifts me up off the ground, and I kick at his thick chest with my sneakers. It's as though I'm nothing more than an insect. There's a rush of air, and for a brief moment, I dimly think I've managed to fly away. I pinwheel my arms. But then, the ground rushes up and I crash into the sand.

Pain lances through my shoulder, then finally settles in my ribs.

Suddenly, the beast that was James is on top of me, his weight making it hard to breathe. *No, no, no!* Wetness trickles down my cheeks. *Am I crying, or is it his drool?* There's a strange keening sound coming from my mouth. I shut my eyes tight.

For a moment, I think of the world as it would exist without me. I imagine Geoff will take over the cafe, filling it with his artwork, the walls adorned with landscapes and the occasional portrait of me. My patrons would look at it and shake their heads. *He had so much potential.* Would Geoff warp reality to get sympathy? *We got back together before he died. We were planning our wedding.* I miss Geoff. I miss tracing the constellations of his freckles and watching him mix oil paint with turpentine. He would often bring the palette to me and ask if a blue shade was morose enough.

And Candy! She's still so rudderless. She needs me. Just last week, she came to my bungalow in hysterics, mascara streaming down her cheeks. "I miss mom," she cried, throwing herself into my arms. "I know it's stupid. But today, I just really missed mom." I held her until she sagged against my chest, arms strung loosely around my neck. Then, I let her sleep in my bed and told her stories about when she was little before mom's hair fell out. *How will Candy survive without me? Who will she hug when she misses me?*

Yip! James is ripped off of me, and I crack my eyelids open. He's baring his teeth at another wolf-creature, this one a stark white, somewhat smaller than James. With the firelight behind them, the difference in size and bulk is much more apparent. They clash in a cacophony of snarls and growls.

I scrabble backward in the sand, digging my heels in. The white wolf clamps its jaws on the other's neck, wrenching it violently from side to side. James loses his balance, and claws at his captor's muzzle to right himself. The two beasts separate and circle one another, fur bristling and chests heaving. The white wolf shakes its head, spraying globules of blood in a wide arc. One of the droplets falls onto my chin.

I can't stay here, I admonish myself, continuing my climb up the steep dune. *Run!*

James leaps at the white wolf again, but it is ready for him. With a great roar, it slams its fist into the side of James' head, knocking him off his feet. An arc of sand showers over me.

Run! I scream, inwardly.

The victor turns its bloody muzzle toward me, slowly walking in my direction.

"You're hurt," the wolf says in a throaty tone. A voice that sounds familiar, but I can't quite place it. I can't *think*.

I continue crab-walking backwards, inching up the side of the dune. I kick sand at the wolf-creature, and it pauses. It drops to all fours, whining.

I remember James' grip on my neck. *Have I been stabbed?* I touch the area gingerly, and dumbly stare at the thick blood on my fingertips. *Oh. yes, I'm bleeding to death.* My head spins, and I double over to retch.

A soft arm encircles my shoulders. "You'll be okay," the same voice soothes.

I *do* know that voice.

Angus! Angus? How did he get here?

"There were wolves!" I cry out. "Wolves!" I am suddenly very aware of the searing pain in my neck, the way it throbs with every subsequent heartbeat, drumming faster and faster.

"I know," he says, resting his cool, calloused palm against my ravaged skin. "We need to get up now. Then I can take you home." He urges me to my feet, keeping pressure on my wound.

"He—it—*I don't know*—said you're married," I babble as we climb the dunes. It's a stupid thing to worry about. I could have died, but I want him to reassure me. I stare at my feet. *Don't fall. Don't fall.* Cresting the dune, I slump in exhaustion. It's like I've been in the ocean, dragged down by a riptide. *I'm tired of swimming*, I think.

"It's okay," he says gently.

It's not okay! How could any of this be okay? Grey motes dance in the corners of my vision, and I try to blink them away. I spit a glob of saliva onto the sand, trying very hard not to puke again.

"Promise not to scream," Angus urges thickly.

"Okay," I mumble. But when I turn to look at him, I can't keep my promise. I scream until I am out of breath. I scream until I cannot scream any more.

CHAPTER FIVE
(ANGUS)

————◁◆▷————

H unter's bungalow is the one with the Adirondack chair. The paperback balancing on the arm, its pages ruffled by sea air, is a thick Stephen King novel. *The Outsider*. His scent is particularly strong there. The pages are dog-eared with a sharp crease. He licks the pad of his thumb when turning pages.

The door is locked, so I put him in the chair, resolving to find a way inside. He passed out when he saw me in this form and has yet to rouse himself. I pad on all-fours around the side of the bungalow, crouching beneath the neighbors' windows to avoid being spotted. I don't want to alarm a resident taking a midnight piss or getting a glass of water from the kitchen.

Finally, I find a window that Hunter has left unlocked. It's small, but I might be able to fit if I am meticulous.

Slowly, I inch the window open and clamber inside. I'm in a kitchen, the porcelain cool under my paw pads. The house is dark and quiet. I must bend at the waist to duck through door frames, and I wince when I realize I've tracked blood inside. The bungalow's floor plan is a mirror image to Ama's but lacks the clutter.

Hunter's walls are painted with bright colors—blues, greens, even oranges—and are adorned with artwork. Some are paintings. Others are photographs. Most are nature shots, but there are a few portraits. In this one, a sepia toned Hunter looks pensive outside of Ebb and Flow. In another, he stands with his arm slung around another man, his mouth agape with laughter. The other man presses his lips against Hunter's apple red cheek.

As I creep through the living room, I'm met with a *hssss!* A cat stares back at me, its tail puffed in fear. I crouch down, holding my furred knuckles out for the cat's inspection. He sniffs me and yowls, then retreats into a bedroom.

Finally, I unlock the front door and peek outside, to make sure the street is still quiet. Hunter is just where I had left him, but he's mumbling now; he's coming to. I heft him up, cradling him against my furred chest.

"A wolf," he mumbles, my fur sticking to his wet lips.

I place Hunter on the couch. Then, I step out of my wolfishness. It's better if he sees me as a human, albeit a naked one, rather than a wolf. I gently turn his head so I can examine the wound at the nape of his neck, clicking on the lamp. There are three shallow punctures in a staggered pattern. *James was playing with him.*

My jaw tightens, and my teeth scrape together with a squeal. *I'll deal with him later.*

Hunter suddenly wakes, swatting at the air with open hands. "Get away from me!" he cries. I sit back on my heels, waiting for him to realize where he is. He sits up, surveying his surroundings with a sigh. "Where—" he begins, slumping his taut shoulders. Then he notices me. He flattens against the back of the couch. "Get away," he squeaks. "Get away from me!"

"Please let me explain," I whisper, afraid that if I'm more overt he will be afraid. Or rather, *more* afraid.

"No, no, there's no way you can explain." He touches the back of his neck, wincing. His fingers come away smeared with blood. "This is a bad fucking dream."

"Hunter, I—" But, I'm not sure what to say. *I'm sorry? I'm sorry I'm a monster. I'm sorry I unintentionally put you in danger. I'm sorry.*

"Get out," he says, his voice strangely calm. His eyes are vacant as though his psyche's somewhere far away, behind a locked door.

I sigh and rise. "I'm sorry," I say hoarsely. "I really am."

He avoids my eyes as I leave. I am careful to shrug into my pelt when I am out of sight. But I can't bring myself to go home. My mouth still tastes of James' blood, and miniscule strands of silvery hair are knotted between my teeth. Harsh reminders of my inability to make tough decisions, especially when it comes to James. After the murder, I should have cast him out of the pack and left him behind. Or I should have euthanized him like a rabid animal.

Every police siren—real or imagined—makes my heartbeat quicken. I throw clothes and toiletries into a bag, ignoring James' prolonged sighs and the sound of his body flopping stomach-first onto our bed. He watches me with an almost bored detachment. As I stand before the cluttered bathroom counter, stowing my toothbrush and razor into a small zip-up travel pouch, he catches my eye in the mirror.

"You're overreacting," he says.

I snort, turning to face him. "I can still smell him on your breath. They have a description—"

"—a vague description."

I brush aside his interruption with a wave of my hand. "A description that is unequivocally you. A description that may very well be backed by security footage any minute now." I toss my toiletries bag into my duffel atop a short pile of clothes. "The autopsy will also show he was fucking eaten."

James sits up, gripping my wrist. "Angus, please."

I wrench my hand away. "I've called Leigh and Luka. They are packing too."

James' face pales at the mention of his twin. He was so ready to toss her aside in the heat of the moment, but now, he can't fathom it. Despite everything, seeing the hurt on his face feels like a lance to the gut. I loved him. No, I love him. He's still my husband. I absently spin the ring on my left hand. I haven't taken it off yet. Despite his threats, despite rutting with another man just two days ago, despite sleeping on the couch, he is still wearing his too.

"Gus," he pleads.

My resolve rips in twain. "Pack your bags," I tell him, my voice steely. "But—" I hesitate, squeezing my eyes shut to quell the encroaching tears. "But, Jay, I'm done." I pull my ring off my finger and toss it to him. "I'm done."

I thought of that moment when I saw the orange glow of the bonfire. I was sitting on the back porch with Ama when the combined shapes of Luke and Leigh crested the hill. When they approach us, both avoid my eyes. Leigh mumbles something about needing to take the cooler inside.

Ama's wolfish ears tip forward toward the beach. "Angus," she says in warning.

Something is wrong. A breeze ruffles my hair, and an amalgam of smells fill my sensitive nostrils: sweat, blood, wolf pelt, charred wood, and *Hunter.*

I jettison out of my chair, only vaguely aware that it had upended in my haste. In less than ten steps, my knees crunch, my spine elongates, and I falter in the thick sand. I manage to right myself quickly, tearing at the loose surface with all four paws. When I finally manage to crest the hill, I look upon a harrowing scene: Hunter, supine on the sand, his fingers tangled in James' fur. James teeth bared; his lips pulled away from his glistening canines. I gallop down the hill, using my momentum to knock James off of Hunter's body. Together, we crash to the ground, sand fanning above our tangled bodies.

Our eyes meet. Mine blue, his black. Time slows. Then, he plunges his nails into my cheeks, dragging them down my snout. The pain is searing, and I palm his snout, pushing his head up and away. With his throat exposed, I lunge, closing my jaws. His heartbeat hammers against my tongue as I squeeze. On his back, he kicks at my abdomen with his powerful hind legs. I squeeze harder.

From the corner of my eye, I see Hunter crab-walking away, tears and snot streaming down his face. Blood trickles down the slope of his collarbone. James stops kicking me, and he puffs his cheeks as he tries, in vain, to pull air into his lungs. He wraps an arm around my maned neck, tapping at my shoulder in a shaky staccato. "Gus," he croaks. The sound of his voice causes something to pop in my core; my resolve fades away.

I let go.

James drags himself out from beneath me, his tail tucked tightly between his legs. He licks at my chin, a gesture of submission. It feels hollow, and I shove him away. He whines and lopes away, back toward the twinkling lights strung across Ama's back porch.

I rush toward Hunter, who is puking into the sand. He is pale and shaking. "It's okay," I soothe, even though I know that, for him, nothing will ever be okay again. His entire perception of reality had been torn asunder.

Moments later, when he screams in my face, my heart shatters.

I doze in the sea grass, but jerk awake when a car pulls up in front of Hunter's bungalow. The porch light turns on as the driver steps out of the car. The man is familiar, but it takes me a moment to recognize him. He was in the coffee shop the day Hunter and I met, his flip-flops slapping against the floor as he followed Hunter to and fro. As the man mounts the steps, the front door eases open, and for a moment, I see Hunter's wan face, his cheeks wet with tears. When they both go inside, the kitchen light turns on, flooding the side yard with light. Through the window, I watch Hunter fall into the man's arms.

CHAPTER SIX
(HUNTER)

⊲◆⊳

After Angus leaves, I lock the door and jam a chair back under the doorknob. I can't stop shaking. Nausea rolls over me in waves, but I think everything in my stomach is splattered across the sand dunes. Still, I retreat to the bathroom to hover over the toilet bowl.

I think of Angus' face, soaked in blood from the nose down, his eyes searching mine. "Please let me explain," he'd said as if he hadn't worn a monster's face mere moments ago.

A *monster*! The word doesn't quite fit. There's something inherently mysterious about monsters; they are amorphous, molded by our individual anxieties. As a child, my monster lived in the crawl space beneath the stairs, seeping through the doorjamb like thousands of ants. But this? This monster was...*real*.

I don't want to be alone. I search for my phone and find it between the couch cushions where I woke up. Perhaps it had all been a dream, after all. But no, my blood stains the neckline of my shirt, and smudged footprints on the floor—a mix of blood and sand—traverse the room. They are far larger than mine.

I call Geoff.

"Hello?" he answers, his voice thick with sleep.

"Can you come over?" I ask, my voice trembling, swallowing the sob that threatens to burst forth from my lips. I press the heel of my palm into my eye socket, making starbursts.

"Are you okay?" Geoff asks, his blankets rustling as he sits up. "You sound weird." I imagine him: his gingery hair mussed, his freckled shoulders sagging.

"No," I manage. "I'm not okay. I saw…" I pause, unsure how to describe what I've experienced. "I saw a wolf."

"Hunt, we live in Virginia," he murmurs. "There are no wolves here."

"Geoff. Just…please come. I need you." I am pleading now, my voice high; it sounds peculiar, not quite my own. As the shadows shift across my living room, I find myself wishing I could dissolve into the couch cushions.

He sighs, the mattress groaning as he gets out of bed. "Okay, okay. I'll be there in five."

While I wait, I sit in the darkness, staring at the front door, too afraid to turn any lights on. If *it* is outside, it will see me. I finger the handle of a butcher knife that I took from the knife block in the kitchen. I've never used a knife on anything more dangerous than a chicken cutlet before. It makes me feel better, though.

The crunch of gravel and the twin beams of light across the room make me leap to my feet. It's Geoff. He's in his pajamas. Slouchy, flannel pants sit low on his hips, a shirt with Andy Warhol's psychedelic Campbell's soup can emblazoned on it.

"You're bleeding," he says, guiding me inside, flipping on the light. "What happened?"

"The wolf," I mumble, allowing him to lead me to the kitchen. For a moment, Geoff disappears into my bathroom, retrieving the first aid kit.

"Sit down, let me see," he says when he returns, gesturing to the kitchen table. Instead, I throw my arms around his neck, sobbing into his shoulder. The knife in my hand clatters to the floor. "Hey," he soothes, rubbing my back. "Hey, babe, I'm here now. You're okay." I cry until I'm exhausted, and his shirt is soaked. Geoff waits patiently until I am done. "Let me look," he prompts, guiding me into a chair with gentle, but firm hands. He examines the wound, gently blotting away the drying blood with a paper towel soaked in warm water. "Tell me what happened."

"I was invited to a thing—a party. But when I got there, this guy attacked me. He said I was messing around with his husband..." Geoff's hands still. "I didn't do *anything*. I met the guy two or three times," I continue. Geoff returns to his ministrations, spreading some sort of salve that smells faintly like maple syrup. "Then, the guy, he.... turned into a wolf."

"Like a *werewolf*?" Geoff asks, incredulous. He pats a rectangular gauze pad onto the nape of my neck, securing it with medical tape. "Hunt, werewolves aren't real." His tone is measured, soft, like I'm teetering on the edge of a long drop, and he doesn't want to startle me.

"I know that," I insist. Geoff pulls a chair close, his brows furrowed. *He doesn't believe me.* But do I even believe it myself? My body feels hot and inert. *Maybe this is all a fever dream. Maybe the weeping punctures beneath my bandage are a dream, too. No.* Geoff's hand touching mine is tangible—the vague memory of Angus' furred chest and the thump-a-thump of his heart as he carried me home is real, too. *He was so soft.*

"Maybe you were drugged?" Geoff suggests. "Did you drink anything at the party?"

I think of the bottle of beer Leigh pressed into my hand. She had already opened it, and water vapor trickled from the top. *Had I taken a drink?* "I don't remember," I say. Geoff leans close, his nose nearly touching mine. He's examining my pupils, looking for the telltale signs of drugging. He smells *really* good, *familiar.* "But," I stammer. "My neck…"

"I'm not saying you weren't attacked. It just wasn't a wolf-man or whatever. You should consider reporting this to the police."

The thought of repeating my bizarre story to a bored-looking police officer sounds unbearable. Surely, they will think I'm insane. Even Geoff, the man I've spent the entirety of my young adulthood with, is looking at me with something akin to trepidation. And I'm so, *so* tired. "Maybe tomorrow."

Geoff glances at his watch. "It's 2 a.m. Let me tuck you into bed, and I'll return in the morning—"

"No," I interrupt him in a panic. "Can you stay? Just for tonight."

"Sure," he says, pushing his wire-rimmed glasses up his nose. Ghost appears in the doorway, his tail flicking. *Meow,* he says coolly, spotting his former owner. He pads toward us, tangling his body around Geoff's legs. Absently, Geoff reaches down to scratch the dip between the feline's shoulder blades. "Let's go to bed, then."

I rise and lead the way to the bedroom. As we cross the living room again, Geoff spots the smears of blood on the carpet. "Are you sure you don't have any more wounds?" he asks.

It must be Angus' blood, but I take a quick inventory, nonetheless. My body is sore, but my neck is the only spot that feels agonizing. Even now, the pain is acute, worsening every time I turn my head. "I'm sure," I mumble. "Maybe my neck bled more than I thought."

I don't tell him about Angus' bleeding muzzle on the beach or the way the blood trickled down his chin when he said, *please let me explain.* Geoff would disregard it as a side effect of some mind-altering drug. But I hadn't felt drugged; my veins were flooded with adrenaline, but my mind was—*is* undoubtedly clear.

In the bedroom, I strip out of my clothes, wincing when the collar of my shirt brushes against my bandage. In my underwear, I crawl into bed, pulling a pillow to my chest. Geoff flips on the light, and I squint my eyes. "Are you sure you want me to stay?" he asks seriously.

"Turn off the light," I reply. "Come to bed. Please. I... don't want to be alone."

Geoff does as he's told, slipping into bed beside me and placing his glasses on the nightstand. He is careful not to touch me. After a long while, his breathing becomes even; he's fallen asleep.

I stare into the inky darkness, too afraid to close my eyes. I imagine a large silvery wolf prowling around my home, sniffing at the cracks, pawing at the foundation. Angus had broken in. Surely, his husband could, too. I leap out of bed, resolving to check all of the windows and doors.

"Where are you going?" Geoff mumbles sleepily.

"The windows," I reply, testing the two in the bedroom.

They are locked, but I'm not convinced they will keep a motivated person or animal out. I press my palms against the glass. *It's thin. Why is it so thin?* Outside, the branches of the river birch scratch the window pane, and I take a step back, startled. The peeling, paper-thin bark flutters, sounding like the long, thick fur on Angus' chest as it brushed against my clammy, tear-streaked cheek. *I didn't imagine it. I didn't imagine him.*

"Let me do it," Geoff says gently. "Get back in bed." He throws the covers back and rises, rubbing the crust of sleep from his eyes. He treads into the living room, and I sit on the edge of the bed. Affection swells in my belly as I listen to him walk through the house, checking windows and doors. He murmurs softly to Ghost, and the cat offers him a mew in return. "All locked," he announces when he returns.

"Okay," I say, relieved. We return to the warmth of the bedsheets and lay face-to-face. It's dark, but I can still make out his features: a rectangular jaw, a faint scar on the bridge of his straight nose, and large, round eyes with thick lashes that make him appear perpetually debauched. I can't help it. I reach out and gently stroke the soft spot just behind his ear. I used to like to kiss him there. "Geoff," I whisper.

"Hmm?" he asks as I cup his face, stroking his fuzzy sideburns with my thumbs. He is careful not to touch me, but he doesn't shrug me off either.

"I—" I stammer, but the words tangle atop my tongue. I swallow. "Thank you. For coming tonight."

"Of course," he replies as though my gratitude is absurd. "I'm always here for you. You know that."

Touching him is like throwing an anchor overboard. The waves of panic settle. Without thinking, I kiss him. His stubble scrapes against my chin. Geoff rears back, searching my eyes.

"Hunter," he warns. "You said that we're over, remember?" Despite himself, his hand rests on my hip, his thumb drawing lazy circles on my skin.

"I know that," I whisper. "Can't we just...." It sounds stupid to say aloud, but I press onward. "... pretend? Just for tonight." I run the rough pad of my thumb, calloused from countless scaldings, along his lower lip. Forgetting himself, the tip of his tongue tips out of his mouth, giving me a gentle lick.

"Just tonight?" he asks breathy.

"Yeah," I murmur, kissing his parted lips again. "I need you tonight."

Without another word, Geoff kisses me back, our teeth clacking. He rolls on top of me, his hardening cock pressing against my pelvic bone. The weight of him is a comfort; normally, it is a weight dragging me underwater.

I reach between us and stroke him through his pajama bottoms.

He groans into my mouth. Geoff's lips descend to my throat, reddening the sensitive flesh there with the edge of his teeth. "I missed you," he says, pulling down my boxers.

I missed the idea of him. But not *him*, not really. Without meaning to, I think of Angus and the easy way he smiles. And those *eyes*, the color of the ocean on a perfect summer day. I push the thought into the recesses of my mind, focusing on Geoff's roaming hands and the huff of his flared nostrils against my clavicle.

He's stroking his cock, his knuckles butting up against my soft stomach. Then, he spits into his hand, rubs the viscous fluid between my ass cheeks. "Hunt," he breathes, pressing his turgid head against my hole. "Are you sure?" He props himself up onto his elbow, examining my face. "We can stop."

My stiff cock brushes against his wiry public hair, making me shudder. "I'm sure."

With a low moan, Geoff presses inside of me. I wrap my legs around his waist, pulling him deeper into my heat. For a moment, his thickness burns, but my body loosens as he slowly presses in then out. Despite the brick wall between us, mortared by words said in anger, we fit together easily.

I reach between us and stroke myself, watching his face contort as he nears orgasm.

When he finally cums, his mouth opens in a silent howl before he slumps on top of me. "That was so good," he finally says.

"Yeah," I whisper. It did feel good. But it didn't fill the dark hollow inside of me, like I had hoped. Stuck somewhere between here and cloistered inside some nightmare., gnashing teeth doggedly pursue me.

Geoff kisses my mouth, my neck, my clavicle. The trail of kisses ends at the base of my still-hard cock. "I'll make you forget," he promises. As his hot mouth envelops me, I try very hard not to think about the wolf that carried me home.

CHAPTER SEVEN
(ANGUS)

⊲◆⊳

Wolfish, I am tethered to the earth. Sea grass tickles my belly, while granules of course sand shift beneath my paws. Despite the siding and drywall between us, I can hear the hum of Hunters' oscillating fan, the yowl of his cat watching me through the kitchen window, the slap of skin against skin. The latter is like a punch to the gut.

I never had a chance; James set it ablaze.

Fury rolls in my belly like a typhoon.

When the sounds of lovemaking finally end and the bungalow quiets, I rise, shaking off the sand clinging to my fur. Hunter is safe and sound and the sun will be rising soon. My vigil is over.

A seagull, startled, takes flight with an angry squawk. On four legs, I make my way to the shoreline, following the white foam to the dunes, and beyond, the abandoned bonfire. It is dark enough that I don't fear early bird joggers, surfboarders, or fishermen spotting me.

I veer right, toward the twinkle lights of Ama's back deck. When I pass the bonfire, I pause, pressing my nose against the sand. I can smell Hunter here: his fear, acidic, and his blood, galvanic like true north. Before I can stop myself, I lap a droplet off the sand, letting it sit on the back of my tongue. *God*. It's as delicious as sex. The wolfish part of me wants to roll in the sand, coating myself in the remains of my triumph.

But I continue onward to Ama's back porch, shrugging off my wolfishness with a shudder. The wound on my face sears, the pain exacerbated as my facial structure shifts from wolf to man.

Before my fingers touch the backdoor's rusting lever handle, I hear James. He's loud, his words obfuscated by peals of his own laughter. *He's drunk*. The others too: snickers, murmurs, even a chuckle. Liquid heat pools in my belly, bile burning a hole. I am very certain if I walk inside and confront him, I may very well kill him. He attacked Hunter purely to hurt me, proving he is unequivocally rabid, surely infected by some sort of prion.

The man I married would never behave like this. The man I married would have never eaten someone in the back of a luxury car, either.

I creep inside and into the bedroom, dressing in a tee and a pair of silken basketball shorts. I want to speak to Hunter if he'll let me. Maybe in the daylight I'll be divorced from the beast he'd encountered last night. Before I leave, I step into the bathroom to wash the brown, flaking blood off of my face, the water turning salmon. There's two deep divots in my cheeks from James's claws, a gruesome Glasgow smile. I wince, patting at the weeping wounds with a fistful of toilet paper. *So much for not looking scary.*

When I step outside—thankfully sight unseen—the sky is a dusky purple, with a paint stroke of pink on the distant horizon.

Before I can leave, the door opens and closes behind me. It's Ama, dressed in a long, silken night-gown. "Is your human okay?"

He's not mine. He will never be *mine*. Not after last night. "He's safe," I reply.

"Your husband has been drinking since he got home," Ama observes coolly. "He's a problem."

"I know," I murmur. "I'm sorry. I don't know what to do."

Ama eases into a chair, folding her hands in her lap. She sits up ramrod straight as if proud her spine isn't bent like the others her age. Her eyes meet mine. Like mine, hers are blue, albeit a true cyan like a summer sky. They are clouded with cataracts, but striking, all the same. "In my day," she begins. I expect her to remind me that James' behavior is punishable by death.

Instead, she tells me a story.

"We met when I was twenty years old. It was the thirties, and we were about to go to war, you know. His name was Bernard Miller. Bernie. I was in secretarial school, and he was enlisting after attending Fordham. He, of course, didn't know what I was. I hid it like a bruise on my thigh. It was unsightly, unladylike. I spent a long time pretending."

"Before he shipped out, Bernie asked me to marry him. I said, *yes.* That night, I told him what I was. I *showed* him what I was. *The poor thing!* He went to Germany. H   e came home shell-shocked. I still wonder if it was my fault, more so than the war. Maybe…I broke him."

"Why are you telling me this?"

"The human isn't capable of what you're asking of him. He'll do his best to forget you. Maybe he'll get hypnosis or turn to drugs. Or he'll end up like Bernie: salivating in a hospital after frying his brain. Leave him alone."

"What about James?" I ask. *How do I even respond to what she's told me?* Sure, it's a sad tale, and it makes my heart hurt for her. But I can't quite give up on Hunter. Not yet. He deserves to know what he'd witnessed, what he'd experienced. And there's a miniscule part of me that wants him to want *me*, despite everything.

"That's a decision for you to make." she says dispassionately. "But, Aggie, you're an Alpha. Sometimes, you must do the absolute worst to make things right."

I think of crushing James' throat between my teeth, shaking the life from him. At the bonfire, I thought I could do it. But then he said my name. *Gus.*

Slowly, Ama rises. "I'll leave you to it. Hopefully, the pups have fallen asleep, so I can get some rest."

After she heads inside, I slip my feet into a pair of discarded flip-flops on the back porch. They are too big for me, either belonging to James or Luka. On the short walk down Bird's Nest, I wrack my brain for something—*anything* I can say to ease Hunter's mind. *I won't hurt you* sounds so trite. And, I *had* hurt him, indirectly.

When I approach his bungalow, I hesitate. Geoff's car is still parked in the dirt drive. Then, the front door opens. It's Geoff, a self-satisfied smile on his face, and a slice of toast loosely wrapped in a paper towel in his hand. He's still in pajamas.

He spots me loitering on the sandy road. "G'morning," he says cheerfully. "It's a nice day, isn't it?" Even when speaking to me, his eyes slide away. I'm inconsequential. He fiddles with his keys.

"Yeah," I respond gruffly. "Suppose so."

The sky is swollen with stratus clouds, many of which are grey. It will surely rain today; with the wind coming off the ocean, it'll be quite chilly. It won't be a nice day at all. Perhaps a night with Hunter is akin to a perfect summer day: salt air, wet heat, feet in the water, and a melting ice cream cone.

I offer him a half-hearted wave, and continue onward, planning to turn back when his car passes.

Behind me, I hear him press the button on his key fob ("beep!") and slide inside his sedan. He coughs, then the keys jingle as he slides one into the ignition. The engine purrs and revs, and he pulls out of the drive. His car passes on my left, and I catch a brief glimpse of his sunglasses in the rearview and a WB bumper sticker. Wharton Beach.

Usually, only tourists plaster those on their cars as if to say, *look where I've been!*

There's a light on inside Hunter's bungalow. As before, the cat perches on the windowsill, the curtain draped over its shoulders like a mozzetta. When the cat spots me, his tail flicks and he rises, stretching until his spine bows. He leaps out of sight, presumably to alert his owner of an intruder. Or, rather, to ask for his breakfast.

For a long time, I stare at the front of the house, trying to sort my thoughts. The white shiplap has turned dingy, from the sun and salt. The rooftop is dotted here and there with clumps of herbaceous matter: seagull nests. As I dawdle, a seagull emerges from behind the eaves, opening its wings. It remains poised there for several moments, waiting for a warm thermal to carry it into the heavens.

I'm stalling.

Tentative, I rap my knuckles against the door. My stomach drops when I hear footsteps inside. Part of me had hoped no one would be home. But then, he opens the door. Hunter looks as though he hasn't slept at all, his eyes sunken and red-rimmed. A suck bruise adorns his pale throat, courtesy of Geoff, I would imagine. The nape of his neck is covered in a thick bandage, held in place by strips of opaque medical tape.

One of the strips flutters, having come undone. I catch myself reaching toward him to reattach it.

"No," Hunter says, taking several steps inside. "No, no, no." *He thinks I've come to attack him.*

"Hunter," I whisper, afraid that if I am too loud, he will flee. "Please, can we talk?"

"You, you... you're a monster," Hunter hisses as though we share a secret.

"It's not like that. Please. I—" But he cuts me off with something akin to a snarl.

"Get away from me, Angus. Geoff is coming back. He'll—"

I sigh, raising my arms, palms forward in surrender. I step backward until I am off the porch and standing in Geoff's tire tracks. The treads made the ground uneven, and I nearly lose my balance. "I just want to talk," I plead. "Really. I can explain."

A hollow laugh bursts from him. "Oh yeah?" He rips off his bandage, tossing the soiled fabric at my feet. The blood soaking it has turned a murky brown, oily with some sort of ointment. "How are you gonna explain *this?*"

I can't. *I can't.* We stare at each other, silent. Even now, his smell is intoxicating. But there's something else too, something *metallic*. "Hunter," I murmur. "You're bleeding."

In his fit, he had ripped the scab from his wound. He touches it gingerly with his fingertips, staring at the blood before wiping it on his *Wharton Annual 5k* t-shirt. The coppery smell is as potent as a glass of grain alcohol and my head swims. My stomach clenches.

"It's fine," he snaps before stepping back inside. "Go home, Angus." He pauses. "Better yet, *leave* my fucking town."

After he slams the door shut, I'm on autopilot. I don't realize where I've gone until I've arrived. My knees butt up against the pullout couch in Ama's living room, my husband snoring on the uneven mattress. There's a line of ragged punctures on his neck. Most of the fight is a blur, except for the lightning strike that was his claws tearing my face asunder.

I can feel my heartbeat in my cheeks, an incessant pounding that threatens to usurp all of my other senses.

Watching James for signs of life, I undress, neatly folding my clothes and putting them aside. Wordlessly, I step into my wolfish flesh, wincing when my snout elongates and the scabs on my cheeks rip open anew. Blood soaks my white mane.

When I am entirely wolfish, I leap atop the sleeping man. "Who—" he manages before I clap my large hand over his mouth and nose.

"I don't want to hear you speak right now," I growl. James can't breathe. He struggles under my hand. When I finally deign to lift my hand, he still can't escape; I'm straddling his hips, and right now, I easily weigh thrice what he does. "If you ever touch Hunter again, I will kill you myself," I continue. "You can't fuck someone else, then get upset when I move on."

Despite his current predicament, James chuckles. "Gus, you really think that human will be yours? You're fucking delusional. I was doing you a favor."

I bare my teeth at him. A globule of saliva drips onto his cheek, sliding down his jaw. "Fuck you," I snap.

James reaches up and strokes my muzzle. "We're meant to be together—you and me. I know I messed up with Nedry. But, baby, I love you." He may as well have kicked me in the stomach. *Oomph.* It's the first time he's said it since we left Portland.

I clamber off of him, squatting on my haunches. "That's not fair," I murmur.

James sits up, propping himself up on his palms. "I know. Come to bed, Gus."

CHAPTER EIGHT
(GEOFF)

———◁◆▷———

I stride down the back alley toward Ebb and Flow, eager to grab some clothes and head back to Bird's Nest, the bungalow, and Hunter. Using my phone, I cancel the classes I'm scheduled to teach with a mass email, feigning illness.

I don't feel safe without you, Hunter had said, his eyes crusty with sleep and unshed tears. *The wolf— he'll come back.*

Werewolves! Jesus fucking Christ. I had wanted to laugh at the absurdity, first believing it a ruse, an excuse to bring us together. Hunter is, after all, a die-hard romantic. What's more romantic than standing back-to-back, fighting a shared enemy? What's more romantic than falling into the arms of a strong, white knight?

The alley is several degrees colder than the parking lot, and gooseflesh crawls up my bare arms. The back of Ebb and Flow is a muted yellow, the heavy door propped open by a weathered cinder block. Inside,

I can hear running water, the clink of dishes, and Emmanuel humming a melody I can't quite place. I unlock the neighboring door, clomping up the stairs in my Birkenstocks.

Candy isn't in the loft, and for that I am immensely grateful. I'm not quite sure what to say to her—not yet. *Your brother is fucking insane.* No, no. That's not right.

I've been living out of a suitcase since Hunter and I broke up. I paw through the tangle therein, selecting a pair of jeans and a fresh t-shirt. I strip, eager to finally remove my flannel pants. It was embarrassing walking through the parking lot in pajamas. *A walk of shame.*

Dressed, I stuff a few outfits into my leather briefcase. Hunter bought it for my thirty-seventh birthday. The leather is caramel-colored, supple, and stamped with my initials: GH. Geoffrey Hawkins. For a moment, I consider bringing my entire suitcase, but I don't want Hunter getting the wrong idea. Conversely, I don't want to give myself the wrong idea, either. It would be so easy to bring my things, hang my shirts back up in his closet, and start calling him "babe" again.

The front door opens, and Candy strolls in. "Oh, hey!" she says in surprise. "I forgot my water bottle. Where were you? I got up to pee last night and you were gone."

I wince. "Hunter's."

Forgetting her task, Candy sits on the couch so that we are eye-to-eye, resting her elbows on her knees. "Are you getting back together?" Her excitement is palpable, making her voice squeak.

I want to remind her I didn't want to break up. But he made it impossible not to; it was like drowning in stagnating lake water, my lungs full of thick algae. His resentment wasn't quiet. It was evident in every sigh, every slammed door, every rebuff.

"Cay, I'm worried about him," I reply carefully. "He called me last night, freaking out, crying about seeing a wolf—a werewolf."

"Y'know, he used to have terrible sleep terrors when we were kids," she muses. "One time, he hit me with a pillow because he thought I was a crocodile."

"He was very insistent that he saw it." I sit back on my heels, fingering the strap of my bag. Candy's brow furrows and I press on. "I think he's having a breakdown."

"He was fine yesterday," Candy replies. "Are you sure it wasn't a dream?"

"You're not listening to me. Hunter said it *attacked* him. He was bleeding all over the carpet. He said he was at some party, and he was attacked by a fucking werewolf! I think he's doing drugs or something."

"You're not fucking with me, are you? This isn't funny, Geoff."

"I'm not," I insist. "I got him cleaned up and calmed down, but he needs help. Professional help."

"Yeah, yeah, of course." Candy's hands shake with unfettered consternation as she taps on her phone screen with her thumbs. "I'll call dad, the doctor, someone. Should I call Hunter? I should call him."

This—all of it—is several echelons above my pay-grade. We aren't even together anymore. There's a part of me that wants to back away, let Candy take the helm. He's *her* brother. In truth, I'm feeling hurt. No matter how he spins it, Hunter was very clearly seeing someone else. *He said I was messing around with his husband.* The words have been tumbling around in my head since he uttered them, even while we were having sex. *Messing around, messing around, messing around.*

"Let me see how he is, and we can figure out what to do, okay?" I finally say. I *do* love him. *God, I love him.*

Candy nods her assent. When I rise, slinging my bag over my shoulder, she grasps my hand. "I feel so useless. What do you need from me?"

"I barely slept, Cay. A cup of coffee would be amazing."

Downstairs, Candy brews a fresh pot of coffee. I rest my elbows on the countertop, watching her work. I wonder as I often do, whether Candy or Hunter is the progenitor of their various idiosyncrasies. They are so very much alike, even though they are several years apart. It makes staying at Candy's both a comfort and a curse. The other night, when Candy huffed at my shoes haphazardly discarded, I could have sworn it was Hunter expressing his displeasure.

I give her a tight smile when she hands me the cup. "I'll call you," I promise.

"Can I get an iced coffee with a splash of soy?" a familiar voice asks.

It's the man I saw outside of my—*Hunter's*—bungalow just an hour ago.

I hadn't recognized him. I had barely looked. But now, I realize where I've seen him before: here, making fuck-me eyes at Hunter. He's wearing a jacket with the lapels up, a scarf loosely wrapped around his mouth and nose. It's not cold enough for it, and he looks absurd. Still, even with half his face obscured, he is objectively attractive. *Is he more handsome than I am? Does he keep Hunter's attention better than I do?*

The man unfolds his wallet and pulls out his debit card, and I notice the letter "J" tattooed on his ring finger. *He said I was messing around with his husband.* An image of Hunter in the arms of this handsome man comes to mind, his eyes half-lidded. I can almost hear the little whimpers that emanate from his parted lips when he's touched *just so*.

I take a sip of my coffee and give Candy a little wave. *I can't stay here anymore. Is it just my imagination, or is the man pointedly avoiding my eyes?*

◆ ◆ ◆

Hunter is in the kitchen when I let myself into the house. I try to ignore the butcher knife clutched tight in his shaking hand. "Geoff!" he breathes, slowly sliding the blade back into the block. "You scared me."

"Sorry," I wince. "I should have knocked."

When we lived together, I made it a habit of quietly letting myself in. I would ease the key into the keyhole, turning it just enough to disengage the lock. *Click.* I liked to see Hunter in his natural habitat, entirely uninhibited. Inconspicuous, I would sidle up behind him and clap my hands over his eyes while crowing, *guess who?* He would nearly always shriek, laugh, then call me an asshole with a playful shove.

Now, he is ready to slide a knife into my gut. A far cry from the man I knew.

Guilt washes over me. I should have been here. If I hadn't moved out, he wouldn't have gone to that party, turning into a tight bundle of nerves.

"Oh!" he exclaims. "Aren't you supposed to be at work? I thought you were..." Hunter trails off, biting his lower lip. He must know he sounds insane.

"A wolf?" I can't seem to temper my querulous tone. *I hope he doesn't notice.*

He turns away, sniffling. "Yeah." His cheeks redden.

I wrap my arms around him. "I took off work," I say gently. "I thought it would be nice to spend the day together."

"You're babysitting me," Hunter observes coolly. "You don't have to do that. I'd rather you not." He is stiff in my arms, but he doesn't shrug me off. His face is pinched, sickly pale.

I stroke his cheek with my knuckles. "I'm not," I reply. "I just want to be here. My lecture on Eugene Von Bruenchenhein can wait."

"Sounds riveting," he remarks dryly, but then he finally relaxes in my arms. The bandage on his neck has come undone; with gentle fingers, I press the adhesive against his flesh. It doesn't stick.

"Come on," I urge him gently. "Take a shower and I'll get this rebandaged." He lets me steer him to the bathroom, and I turn on the shower for him, waiting for the water to warm. The skylight makes the room bright and hot, and the wet heat from the shower makes it humid, too.

As he undresses, I turn away, averting my eyes. Twelve hours ago, I was inside of him. But now...I feel *awkward*.

While he showers, I look through the clothes in our—his!—closet. I select a pair of cozy sweatpants and an Ebb and Flow t-shirt, then place them on the bed. Hunter pads into the bedroom, naked, drying his hair with his towel. I am struck by how comfortable he is with me. It's as though our hiatus was just that: a hiatus. Something finite; a *see you later,* rather than a *goodbye*.

"What?" he asks. I'm staring.

"Nothing," I reply quickly. Too quickly. He raises his eyebrows. "I got you some clothes to…uh, wear," I sputter.

"Thanks." Hunter steps into the sweatpants and pulls them up his legs. His ass jiggles as he pulls the waistband up over it. *Fuck*. I used to be able to touch him whenever I'd like. I want to fill my hands with him.

"How are you feeling?" I ask.

"Oh, you know," he replies, pulling the shirt over his head. "Just feeling like a crazy person." His still-damp hair sticks up, mussed by the fabric.

"You aren't—" I offer, but I can't bring myself to finish the sentence. He may very well be crazy. He *sounds* crazy. "You must admit: it's far-fetched."

Hunter's lips press together, and he clicks his tongue. "You don't think I realize how I sound?" His verdant green eyes— bright and defiant—meet mine. "I know what I saw. I know what happened to me. You don't have to be here, you know."

"I want to be," I insist. "Come sit down. Let me put medicine on your neck." I gently take his hand, leading him back into the bathroom. I open the fogged mirror, revealing the medicine cabinet recessed in the wall and reach for the first aid kit I had left there this morning. "Sit," I order, gesturing at the toilet.

Obediently, he sits on the closed lid. "Are you sure?" he asks as I tilt his head to squirt a dollop of Neosporin on his neck. The wound is scabby, and the three distinct scratch marks are more prominent. They traverse the nape of his neck, nearly from ear to ear. *He could have done it himself.* I think of the butcher knife, the one he reached for when he was scared.

"Am I sure about what?"

"Are you sure that you want to be here?" he clarifies. He looks up at me with emerald eyes, the same eyes that beguiled me years ago. Those eyes could get me to do nearly everything, except for the one thing he really wants.

I just don't believe him. How could I?

"Of course." I pat a new gauze pad on the back of his neck, taping it to his skin. "All done."

I stay the night. While Hunter fitfully sleeps, rolling to and fro, I lay awake, staring at the ceiling. Ghost meows as he leaps onto the mattress, sniffing at my feet. Somehow, he is inkier than the pitch-dark room. He rubs his cheek against my big toe. Then, he curls up against the curve of my calf, his purrs radiating up my leg. Ghost used to sleep there on the rare occasion he deigned to join us in bed.

It really is nice to be here. Comfortable. Even with Hunter falling apart before my eyes, it feels good to be back in my house, in my bed, listening to him breathe.

I've slept terribly since staying at Candy's. I thought it was because of the thin mattress, but maybe it's because I missed this—him. Us.

I roll on my side, wrapping an arm around Hunter's waist. He stills, settles, his breathing deepening into soft snores. I press my nose against his hair, inhaling. It's a comfort; he smells like the body wash we used to share. I cannot help but imagine the showers we used to take together, soaping each other's backs, asses, cocks. Afterward, still wet, we would tumble into bed, kissing those same spots.

I've slept with a few people since we broke up, but no one compares to him. Though, they never spoke of werewolves, their voices trembling with conviction. It was easier. Simple.

Except, I didn't love them.

CHAPTER NINE
(HUNTER)

───◁◆▷───

I think about calling in sick again. But it's been a week. So, I get dressed, putting on jeans and a hoodie. The latter will hide my wound relatively well; I don't want to discuss what happened. Or rather, I don't want to have to lie about it and have anyone look at me as though I'm deranged. Geoff already looks at me as though I'll rip my clothes off and run naked through the streets.

Geoff stayed over again last night. We watched television and gorged ourselves on paneer tikka masala and aloo gobi. It was as though he'd never moved out, never told me he didn't want to get married.

He is still in my bed when I leave the house, and I almost kiss him before I go. It's purely a reflex. *Isn't it?*

I'm late. Renee texts me as I trot along the pier toward Main Street.

[Renee: Where are you??????]

By the time I reach Ebb and Flow, she's in a rage, pacing back and forth in front of the locked door. "This is why I need a set of keys. Of course, Candy isn't answering her *fucking* phone either," she complains as soon as she spots me. But then, she raises her eyebrows. "Are you okay? You look like shit."

"Thanks," I say wryly.

Renee pulls her hands into the sleeves of her hoodie, shoving them into the kangaroo pocket. "You know I didn't mean it like that," she says. "Can we please go in? I'm fucking freezing."

The rain largely abated overnight, but errant droplets still fall here and there. A fat one lands upon my nose, bursting. I wipe it away with my hoodie sleeve.

"Yeah," I say, unlocking the door. I start putting the chairs under the tables, clinging to the lifeboat that is my checklist. I need something to feel *right*. What happened in the dunes was *wrong*. Even Geoff in my bed, Geoff kissing my lips, Geoff's hands in my hair, feels *wrong*.

"Really though," Renee says, making whipped topping with practiced hands, her sleeves pushed up to her elbows. "Are you okay?"

"Yeah," I say. "Just things with Geoff." That's the part I can verbalize, at least. The rest feels like a fever dream. Something I could've convinced myself hadn't happened if that *werewolf* hadn't hurt me, if Angus hadn't shown up at my house afterward spouting apologies.

Renee stops stirring. "Geoff?"

"He's been coming over," I reply, edging around the counter to rouse the register. Then, I brew a carafe of coffee. The sound of the thin stream of coffee filling the glass container has always sounded soothing, like standing near a water feature in a spa. But it's far less so when Renee is staring at me, her lips set into a thin, tense line.

"Hunter."

"I know."

"Hunter!" She shakes her head, clicking her tongue.

"I know." I sigh. "It's been nice, though. Having him around." Renee rolls her eyes. Suddenly, the door jingles, and Ms. Driscoll shuffles in, her back permanently hunched from osteoporosis. "Hello, Mr. Bailey, Ms. Carmichael."

"Good morning," I tell her, trying to appear cheerful. I can still feel Renee's eyes boring into my back. "What can I get you?"

"Just my usual," Ms. Driscoll says, setting her purse onto the counter. She fishes through it, presumably searching for her wallet. She places a pair of sunglasses, a coin purse, Chapstick, a small handful of peppermints, and a playbill for the 1993 Broadway debut of *Angels in America: Perestroika* on the countertop. "Oh dear," she mumbles. "I must have left it at home. I'll come back later." She repacks her bag, dejected.

"Don't worry about it," I assure her, reaching for the carafe and pouring a cup of coffee. I gesture for Renee to fetch Ms. Driscoll's favorite treat from the bakery case. "It's on the house."

"I don't want to be a bother," Ms. Driscoll murmurs, but she's pleased. Her cheeks are a bright pink, and she preens under my gaze. "You're so sweet, Mr. Bailey!"

"*Hunter*, please. Are you dining in?" I ask, already knowing the answer. Every morning, without fail, Ms.

Driscoll orders a coffee and a thick slice of banana nut loaf. Then, she sits at the table closest to the window, where she observes passers-by and works on a project. This month, she has been teaching herself needlepoint. Often, while busing tables, I'll hear her cursing under her breath as the thin thread inevitably tangles. When she nods, I gesture for her to lead the way. "I'll carry these for you."

After helping Ms. Driscoll, Renee is champing at the bit. "Geoff has been *staying over*?" she hisses in a low voice, so the old woman doesn't overhear.

"Just for a few days," I reply. I wish I hadn't said anything. Renee piles her hair into a loose topknot, but her eyes never leave mine. I'm not going to be able to end this conversation unless I give her some tasty morsel. "I was having a bad night." An understatement. "He came over to comfort me."

"Comfort you, huh?" Renee waggles her eyebrows suggestively. "I bet he did."

A group of off-season tourists—delineated from the general milieu by sunburnt cheeks and beach-wear—walk in, and, thankfully, save me from further inquiry. I make the drinks while Renee mans the cash register. It feels good to be at work, comfortable, even. Thoughts of werewolves fade away.

Candy meanders in mid-morning. She doesn't work today, and I fortify my defenses. "Really, Hunt?" she says without preamble. She is wearing jeans and a ratty band tee, pilfered from her ex-boyfriend, Julien. She's never listened to Van Halen in her life.

"What?" I ask, pouring a slush of espresso and chocolate into a cup. The mixture froths, nearly encroaching on the rim.

"You know what. Geoff has barely been at the apartment. He said he's been staying with you." She rests her hands on her hips, one shoulder cocked.

"I've had a bad few days—" I manage, but she cuts me off. Candy isn't one to mince words, nor beat around the bush. She's clearly already tired of this back-and-forth.

"—Geoff is my friend too, you know," she snaps. "He talks to me. I just don't want you leading him on."

Her words sting. I quell the impulse to shout, *he led me on first!* But had he? He was clear about his wants; it was I who was blinded by my needs.

I press my lips together, handing the drink to Renee so that she can ring it up. "I don't want to talk about this here," I hiss.

"Then lets talk in the back." She gestures around the sparsely occupied cafe. "Ren can handle this. Right, girlie?"

Renee nods, rolling her eyes at Candy's term of endearment. She probably thinks it's so outdated. What do young people call their female friends now? Queen. Fam. Bitch. Sis. Something either uplifting or derogatory, depending on the circumstance.

I sigh, stepping out from behind the counter, following my sister into the backroom. The back door is ajar, held in place by a cinder block, a trickle of cigarette smoke wafting inside. Emmanuel is on his break. I'm glad for it. I don't want to talk about this in front of him, or anyone for that matter.

"Look," I say, "I was attacked by *something* at a party. I asked Geoff to come over because I was scared."

Candy sighs, raking her fingers through her hair. "Geoff mentioned you had a bad dream or were tripping on something."

No! Red hot anger wells up inside of me. How dare he refashion my experience into something palatable. How dare he lay his annoyance at my feet. *I* had a dream. *I* did some party drug and lost my cool.

"I was attacked," I repeat, "by an animal."

"A wolf," she says, unable to disguise her incredulousness. "He said you thought it was a werewolf."

"It *was* a werewolf," I insist. Having the two people I care about most discount me, cuts just as deep as claws plunged into my skin. "I don't care if you don't believe me. I don't care if Geoff doesn't either. It's what I saw."

"Hunt." Candy's cool hand touches my arm. "You really need some help."

"Stop it," I snap, imagining men in white jumpsuits swarming from a white van, carrying nets and a straitjacket. "There's nothing *wrong* with me. You're more concerned about Geoff's feelings than mine." I feel indignant, like a child. I want to stamp my feet.

Candy squeezes my arm. "You're my big brother, and I love you. I just don't want you getting hurt again. You need to get your shit together." She means she wants me to stop talking about werewolves. Just like Geoff, she wants me to accept the simplest explanation rather than an extraordinary one.

It doesn't matter. I know the truth.

"I'm fine," I say tersely, shrugging her off. "I won't lead anyone on. I'm trying to do my job. You have the day off, Cay. Don't waste it here." I brush past her and return to the cafe proper.

"You okay?" Renee asks.

"Fine."

♦ ♦ ♦

It's late afternoon, and the cafe is quiet. While most of the tables are occupied, patrons are thoroughly engrossed in their phones or laptops.

Renee slumps against the counter, her chin resting heavily on her palm. "You really need to hire more baristas," she groans.

I chuckle. "But then, I won't get to spend my days with you."

"You haven't hired anyone since Angie and Lawrence went back to college. It's been *weeks*." *She's right*. I've been distracted by my break up with Geoff.

"I'll put out a 'help wanted' sign," I promise her. "Maybe we can get someone in next week."

"And *I* should get a set of keys," she adds, giving me a pointed look.

The bell above the door jingles. Angus walks in, alone, his hands deep inside his jean pockets. His long hair, typically wild, is tucked behind his ears. "Hey," he says softly, approaching the counter.

Renee straightens, giving him her most luminous customer service smile. "What can I get you?"

"Iced coffee with soy," he replies. "Large."

"Coming right up," she says, glancing at me. But I haven't moved to make the drink. *This is what it must feel like when a rabbit spots a hawk on the horizon.* Renee huffs and begins to make the drink herself, dropping a handful of ice into the blender and switching it on. The sound of ice crunching reminds me of the sound I heard when Angus' husband transformed before my very eyes. It's as though his bones broke and mended themselves into new angles.

"Hunter," Angus says, wary. "Can we talk?" I hate that he's so beautiful. In dark-wash jeans and a black tee, his pale skin looks almost milky. His muscles are well-defined through the fabric, and he towers above me. I can't help but to remember the way he carried me as though I weighed nothing.

"No," I say sharply. "Renee, is that drink done yet? Angus is in a hurry." Renee doesn't answer me. She pours dark roast coffee over the ice.

"If you just give me ten minutes," Angus pleads. "I'll never bother you again. I promise." Renee reaches around me to retrieve the carton of soy milk from the fridge. While she adds the creamy liquid to the coffee and gives it a quick stir, I grit my teeth. *Please hurry, Renee.* Angus' eyes are so soft and I'm having a difficult time saying no. He scares me, but he took care of me, too. Surely that means something.

"Fine," I relent. "After closing. Here."

"Thank you," Angus says. Renee hands him his drink and he hands her a debit card. Now that I've agreed to see him, he avoids my eyes as if worried I'll change my mind. I want to. I should.

Renee leaves just after the last customer, eager to get to the annual Wharton fair. "Are you sure you don't want me to help clean up?" she asks, loitering in the doorway. She bites her lip, eyes darting. "I can be a little late."

I wave her away. "No, no, I've got this. Angus is stopping by before I lock up, anyway, remember? Maybe I'll hand him a broom."

Renee chuckles. "Please don't fuck on the counter, alright? It's unsanitary."

"Renee!" I admonish her. "It's not like that."

"Yeah, you said you'd never get with Geoff again, too." *Ouch.* Renee is so very perceptive, and files ammunition away for later in that conniving brain of hers. Usually, her sights aren't trained on me. In that regard, she and Candy are peas in a pod.

"Go, enjoy the fair." I laugh.

"I'm *going.*" She steps out onto the street and heads toward Wisteria Ave and, beyond it, the pier. It's the first Friday in October, and the fair has returned, like clockwork. Surely, she will be partaking in clandestine beers behind the tilt-a-whirl, rolling her eyes at the tourists.

I like to be in Ebb and Flow alone, after-hours. It's cozy. This building is as much my home as my bungalow is, perhaps even more so. I spent most of my childhood and adolescence here, and after-hours, my mom would perch on the counter and help Candy and I with our homework. My dad would unpack the sandwiches we stored in the swamp cooler in the alley behind the store and divvy them out: ham and cheese for me, peanut butter for mom and Candy, and peanut butter and jelly for himself. I would solve math problems, the sound of pricing guns and mom's airbrush my soundtrack.

The door jingles; it's Angus. "Hi," he whispers, slowly easing into the chair closest to the door. He places his hands on the tabletop, palms down and fingers spread. Each movement seems to have been rehearsed. Combined, the message is clear; *I want you to feel safe.* "Thank you for seeing me." He smiles, or tries to. The deep abrasions bisecting his cheeks makes it look more like a grimace.

"Yeah," I manage. I hate that, despite my fear, I am struck by his countenance. He is looking at me as though I am the sun, and he is a gyrating heavenly body. And, he *does* have a heavenly body. He's changed into a button-up, the sleeves rolled up to his elbows. Two or three buttons are undone, and when he moves, I can just catch a glimpse of kinky chest hair. I should be frightened. I've seen him with fur so white it is almost translucent, fibrous shoulders, snapping jaws, and keen claws.

"I want to apologize," he continues. "I had no idea that James—my *ex*—would do that. It was unconscionable. I'm sure you have a lot of questions."

"Yeah," I repeat. "I don't even know where to begin. Are you a werewolf?" It feels absurd to say the word aloud.

"I suppose you could say that. We can as you've unfortunately seen, become wolves. In most cases, it's genetic. But some are bitten by rabid wolves—sorry, that's just the colloquialism we use—*bloodthirst*y. The wolf you met, the one who attacked you, is, I suspect, rabid." His brow furrows and his hands stiffen into fists.

Slowly, I sink into the chair across from him. It's a small table and our knees touch. My stomach flip flops. "Does that mean…?" I touch the back of my neck. *Will I be a monster, too?*

"No, no. Oh god no. He just scratched you." Forgetting himself, Angus reaches across the divide between us and touches my fingers. "Hunter, you're very pale. Breathe. Everything is okay. I promise."

I nod, dumbly. His fingers are calloused, and his touch is warm. I shouldn't take him at his word. He's lied to me before. *Well*, I amend, *he lied by omission.* Though, I suppose we weren't close enough to tell familial secrets. We barely know anything about each other. I just know that his gaze makes my cheeks burn.

Angus continues, the words spilling out of him in fits and starts: "Most people don't know we exist— beyond legend—and we like to keep it that way. It's a hard thing to explain. I mean, you've *seen* it, and you're still looking at me as though I'm certifiable."

I look down at my hands, our hands. He's still touching me, and I'm not pulling my hands away, either. His thumb slowly strokes mine. "How have you kept this a secret?" I ask.

"My pack all have normal jobs and human friends, and we are only wolfish when we can do so safely. In Portland, where we lived, we used to meet up in the park and hunt deer. Sometimes we would rent a remote cabin in Washington and spend a few days as wolves."

"Your pack?"

"Leigh, Luka, James." Each time he says his name, Angus looks more pained. It's like every utterance of 'James' means another needle under his skin. He must feel like a Cenobite. "Ama is like us, too."

"Why did you leave Portland?" It's the first time he's said where he lived before Wharton. In fact, I explicitly remember his shushing Leigh when she mentioned it.

Angus is stony-faced. "James got into trouble. It was too risky to stay. I knew we would be safe here because Ama is here. I knew she would know what to do." The thought of that tiny, frail woman being the pack's touchstone makes me grin. She's never struck me as someone with power, especially not power with a capital P. It's apparent that Angus respects her; each syllable is imbued with admiration.

"This is surreal," I manage. It's as though each new fragment of information tears at my concept of reality. "Your world must be so different from mine."

"We aren't like you—humans, I mean," he says. "You might see us as barbaric and lawless, but we punish those who expose us. They are cast out or put down like dogs."

I can't help but to think of my family's dog, Charlie, who we had to euthanize after his organs started to fail one-by-one. It was a quiet moment; I remember stroking his flank as his breathing slowed and stopped, as his eyes fluttered closed. I don't think Angus means quite the same thing.

"James should have been put down weeks ago," Angus continues, hanging his head. "He did something horrific in Portland. But I couldn't do it. Then, I should have done it after the bonfire. But—" His jaw clenches and unclenches. "I'm supposed to be strong. I'm the Alpha."

I'm not sure what to say. Angus doesn't strike me as someone who would hurt a soul, much less commit murder. I can see the sense in the practice though: an eye for an eye. In the deepest depths of myself, I think that I would feel better—safer—if James shuffled off this mortal coil. I certainly wouldn't be sad to see him go. *Does that make me a bad person?*

"He said he's your husband," I finally say softly. I'm not quite sure why my heart is hammering. I'm not frightened of him so much as I'm disturbed that he will say *yes, I'm married*.

"He's my ex. We're not legally married, never were. We've been over for a while now," he replies.

We both sit in silence. For a long moment, the only sound is our breathing, out of sync. Outside, pedestrians stroll past, their voices muted. Finally, Angus releases my hands. "I'm so sorry." Abruptly, he rises, tucking his chair back under the table. "I just wanted to explain it to you. As well as I can. I wanted you to know you're safe." He steps toward the door; he doesn't want to overstay his welcome.

"I don't know if I can feel safe ever again." The words spill out of me, unbidden. I hadn't ever tried to verbalize the complicated array of feelings swirling inside of me. I didn't have a chance to. Since the bonfire, I've been reactionary, going through the motions and responding to stimuli.

Angus kneels so that we are eye-to-eye, his eyes cerulean. "I will keep you safe," he promises. His hand rests on my knee.

"Why?" I don't understand why he cares. I'm sure that, to him, I'm as inconsequential as a mosquito. I've seen James, large and intense. I don't compare.

"Hunter, I—" He sighs, eyes darting, before pressing onward. "I really like you."

If this were a normal conversation with a normal man, I would be elated. But here and now? My mind is a jumble. Though, when his hand takes mine and he repeats those words ("I really like you"), my heart soars.

CHAPTER TEN
(ANGUS)

———◁◆▷———

Hunter is remarkable. Despite the inordinate amount of information I've lobbed at him, he's still willing to listen. He's endured horrific things, and he's still looking at me with those beautiful, warm eyes. He smells like the coffee beans he ground this morning: vanilla spice and roasted almond. Beneath the esters of his profession, there's a hint of soap and the clammy, acrid smell of fear. "You like me?" he asks, mystified.

I rest my hand on his knee and feel the muscle twitch violently under my palm. "I've never met someone like you," I reply. "I haven't stopped thinking about you since the moment we met. Hunter, you're beautiful."

Hunter presses his palms against his hot cheeks as though he can hide them from me. 'I've been thinking about you too," he admits.

Tentative, I lean close. His eyes widen. I can't help but to think of how a deer's eyes bulge and roll when they've spotted me in the grass, when they're running for their lives. Or the way their meat tastes when they die scared—sour, spoilt. *Will I always think of sustenance and violence when I'm near him?* His hands drop to his lap. "I really would like to kiss you."

Hunter swallows, his Adam's Apple bobbing. "I—"

Abruptly, I rise. "It's okay," I say, hurriedly. I don't want him to feel pressured. I don't want him to be scared. "I'm going to go," I tell him. "Please know that my ex won't bother you anymore. I'll make sure of it." I turn on my heel with the precision of a soldier and head toward the door. It's dark out, and I can see my reflection in stark relief on the cafe's window. Beyond my pale face and set jaw, I can see Hunter's pinched features and downcast eyes. He clasps his hands, the knuckles turning white.

When I open the door, the bell above the door rattles with a cheery report. The air outside rushes in, and I'm surprised at how cold it is for an October evening. My skin prickles with gooseflesh; it's uncannily similar to the feeling of my fur sprouting. I can see the vague shape of the carousel on the pier, the twinkle lights attached to the rigging oscillating on a fixed axis. I step over the threshold but then—

—Hunter's hand grips mine. When I turn back to face him, surprised, he kisses me. It's chaste, infuriatingly slow; I want to devour him, and it takes everything in me to tamp that instinct down. His lips are soft, malleable. I walk him back into the cafe proper, our hips butting together, shutting the door behind me. I don't want to kiss in the doorway, suspended between two states: coming and going. I don't want to go anywhere. I just want to kiss him.

Hunter pulls away, his eyes meeting mine. "I just…
really wanted to do that. Just once."

"Just once?" I ask, thickly. I rest my palm on the
hard edge of his hip, longing to hook a finger through
his belt loop. *Come here*, I would say. *You're mine*. I'm
not usually like this. It strikes me that I'm behaving
like James, a man obsessed with finery, fighting, and
fucking. I try very hard to push thoughts of my ex
out of my mind, pushing him out of my lungs with a
wavering breath.

"Just once," Hunter repeats. The way his breath
hitches, the rouge in his cheeks, betrays him. I touch
his cheek, stroking the stubbled skin with the pad
of my thumb.

"Once more?" I ask. Outside, the world moves on
without us. But he simply laughs and pushes me gently
out the door. Then, he locks it, meeting my eyes as he
flips the sign from OPEN to CLOSED.

◆ ◆ ◆

The pier is alive; my senses are inundated with
novel sights, sounds, and smells. It's nearly overwhelming. Still, I take my time, meandering through
the crowd, inhaling the scent of frying dough and spun
sugar. I think that I may have been to some iteration of
this fair as a child. I have a vague memory of riding a
Ferris wheel and hugging a foul-smelling teddy bear
my dad had won for me. I see a lot of people who look
vaguely familiar, which is not uncommon in towns
of this size. Most I've passed on the street, seen sunning themselves on the beach, or stood behind while

waiting for coffee. Some work in the grocery store or loiter outside of the local shops. I even see the barista, Renee. She looks woefully bored, a man's arm slung over her shoulders. He leans close to her, excitedly talking into her ear.

"Look who it is," a voice says from behind me, clapping their hands onto my shoulders. It's Luka. He is excited. The pier is full of people his own age. He's probably tired of hanging out with a bunch of uncool thirty-somethings who don't laugh at the memes he adores. "Hey homie," he says.

"Hey, Lu." Leigh and James follow Luka, albeit more slowly. Leigh gives me a tight smile, searching my eyes as if she can discern whether I've forgiven her—them. I haven't. There's a large part of me that wants to cast them all out of Wharton. It would certainly make my life much easier. But a pack is a family.

James is unruffled, though he clearly didn't expect to see me here. "Hey, Gus," he says coolly. He winces and corrects himself, "Angus." I grunt, unable to form the words that would constitute a proper greeting. We had left so much unsaid the night before. He made sure we didn't talk.

"Come to bed, Gus," he cajoles.

I grumble under my breath, stepping off the bed. As a wolf, I take up a considerable amount of space. In the cramped living room, it makes me off-balance, clumsy.

"Run with me?" he asks, hopeful. In moments, we're both loping out of Wharton proper. We pause beneath the shadow of the water tower, catching our breath. James pisses on the supports. Then, we continue onward into the relative safety of the dogwoods.

I smell her first. It's a doe, nibbling at the underbrush about a hundred yards away. Driven largely by instinct, we drop onto our bellies in the dirt. Saliva pools in my mouth.

After a pregnant moment—which feels like eons—James lunges, coursing through the brush on all four legs. I follow. The deer, spotting him, leaps, twisting in midair in a vain attempt to escape. James readily catches her, sinking his teeth into her muscular shoulder. She lets out a strangled blat, kicking at him ferociously. I bite the nape of her neck, my teeth glancing off the curve of her skull. Blood fills my mouth, dripping down my chin.

The doe bucks and James wrenches at the meat of her shoulders, pulling her off her feet. Then, in unison, we rip at her until the shock stops her bleating and, eventually, her heart. I tear a thin strip of meat off of her long, tapered neck. The venison is warm, and I swallow with a shudder of abject ecstasy. James makes happy sounds as he opens her stomach, her intestines coiling around his legs. Looking at him, my heart swells. He is an esteemed hunter—a worthy mate. He wanted to remind me of that.

After we eat our fill, our bellies distended, we head home. Ducking through the threshold, we find the house as dark and still as when we left. I can still hear snoring in the guest room. I slip out of my fur first, shaking off the pins-and-needles, the ache associated with the transformation. I am covered in blood, and I make a beeline toward the bathroom. The water from the shower head is cool, but I step in, scrubbing at my soiled skin until it is inflamed. After a few minutes,

Chapter Ten (angus)

James joins me, slipping into the cramped cubicle behind me.

"James," I warn. But he takes the sliver of soap from my hand and washes my back in great, sweeping circles.

"You've got blood on your back," he says coolly. "You can do mine, too." Seemingly against my will—as if my body is unfettered by my anger—my cock begins to stiffen. His body molds to mine, and as he presses his thumbs into the sore spots on my neck, I sigh. "It was good, wasn't it?" he asks. "Tonight, I mean."

"Yeah," I manage, closing my eyes. I hate that I still love him. Or do I simply love the man who used to occupy this body, the person who hadn't murdered a politician's son? The person who hadn't cheated. The detectives found Nedry with his designer jeans around his thighs. I never asked—I didn't want to hear it—but clearly, they had fucked, right?

"It's euphoric," he continues. "The hunt, sinking your teeth into that warmth for the first time." I think of the strip of skin, fat, and flesh I had torn away from the doe's slender neck. It was like being intoxicated, only the neurons in the hindbrain firing. It was like my paws were rooted into the earth and I could hear the plants speak to one another. I could hear the rabbits in their burrows crying danger, danger, danger is near *as our prey lost her footing. "It's twice as good when it's a man."*

I turn so that we are nose to nose. His expression is unreadable. Droplets of water course down his cheeks, and drip off the tip of his aquiline nose. "James, that was murder."

"Didn't we commit murder tonight?" he asks.

"The deer was food," I reply. *"We are* meant *to eat her."*

"Who says?" James asks. His fingers trail down my abdomen, and I swat them away.

"It's nature," I insist.

"Our ancestors thought it was natural to eat humans, too." James leans close, his lips nearly brushing against mine. "Killing Nedry felt so right. It felt just as invigorating as felling that deer tonight, even more so."

"It's wrong," I snap, *pushing him back against the shower wall. I'm not gentle, and the back of his head cracks against the tile like a thunderclap.*

James laughs, touching the spot. A streak of blood dirties his fingers. "You can be upset about it, Gus, but it's true." The water is cold now. Without soaping my hair, I abruptly open the door of the shower, stepping out into the bathroom proper. Dripping, I search for a towel while James laughs.

"Do you want to come eat with us?" Leigh asks, jerking me from my reverie. "We're going to La Petite Crique." James clearly chose the venue. He loves French fare, or, rather, I suspect he likes *telling* people he likes it. Whenever we would eat at Le Faucon or some other French bistro in the city, he would insist we stop at TILT afterward for a burger and fries ("I'm still hungry," he'd whine, "the plates are always so small. Gorgeously plated and *fantastic,* but I'm a growing boy").

I want to say no. Luka's pleading eyes make me change my mind. He's been very contrite since the bonfire. He even pulled me aside to tell me it was all

James' idea, and had been assured that my ex only wanted to frighten Hunter. I believe Luka. "Sure," I say. They're my packmates after all. *Family.*

The four of us walk abreast through the crowd. The veritable phalanx steps aside for us, and we head down an alley. "Do you know where the restaurant is?" I ask.

"Sure," James replies. It's a lie, of course. James can't help but to lie. The alleys in Wharton are narrow, lined with dumpsters. Most of the buildings with exit doors therein are shops, with fire escapes snaking down from above. We pass a few shopkeepers standing on the fire escape's landings, smoking cigarettes, and chatting across the way. We meander through the alleyway until we end up parallel to Main Street. Then, I see him.

Hunter carries two black trash bags to the dumpster. The bandage on his neck has come off entirely, and I can smell the plasticky odor of old adhesive and the iron of thickened blood. When he lifts the dumpster lid, the smell of him dissipates, replaced by the almost saccharine smell of garbage. Hunter doesn't notice us until we are a few feet away, and he jumps. "Oh," he exclaims. His eyes meet mine, his eyebrows furrowed.

"Look who it is," James says coolly.

"James," I snarl without looking at him. I only have eyes for Hunter. His face is wan and his lower lip trembles. "We're just passing through," I assure Hunter. "I'm sorry."

"You smell like him, you know," James tells me, throwing an arm around my neck and pressing his nose into the space below my jaw. He kisses me there, and I can feel the curve of his smile. He's fucking with me.

109

Hunter abruptly heads toward the door, kept ajar with a brick. He fumbles when he attempts to kick the brick aside, and James chuckles. "Really, Gus, *this* human? It's bad enough he's human, but weak too?"

"I don't know what you're talking about," I reply. Hunter steps inside the relative safety of the cafe's kitchen. "Jay, I thought you knew me better than that," I continue, trying to keep my voice even. "Didn't we have a good time last night?" Hunter casts his eyes downward as he pulls the door shut. I can hear the *click* as he locks the door from the inside. If I've convinced him, then I've surely convinced James. *Right?*

Leigh crosses her arms over her small breasts. "Can we go?"

"Yeah," James says. "We can go. I'm hungry, anyway." He pulls me against his hip, so that we must walk in lock step. He's staking his claim, despite my earlier rebuff. As we continue onward, he tilts his head so that he can speak into my ear. "Are you really into that human?"

I want to say, *he has a name*. I want to say, *yes*. I want to say, *I don't want to see you ever again*. But instead, I snort, wrinkling my nose. "No, of course not." I hope that I sound believable. I want James to lower his hackles.

To my relief, he doesn't probe any further.

We exit the alley at Jefferson Court, walking along the sidewalk. The street is teeming with people, heading to and from various restaurants and bars. Many are dressed in fair garb: glow stick bracelets, marijuana leaf accessories, cheap stuffed animals tucked under their arms, and oversized cowboy hats made of foam. Music emanating from various patios create a cacophony of sound: pop music from The Tailgate, rock 'n roll from Schooners, and contemporary country from Shuckers Taphouse. It's like we have walked into another world, entirely separate from Main Street in space and time. This is where the tourists and locals go to get fucked up and gorge on overpriced cheeseburgers and heaps of French fries.

Le Petite Crique is a diamond in the rough. Once we enter, it's as though the raucousness of Jefferson Court ceases to exist. The tables are draped with crisp white linen, and adorned with miniature lamps emanating a warm, albeit muted, glow. A host leads us to a circular table, and we sit. I make sure to grab the chair between Leigh and Luka, desperate to get away from James to catch my breath and recover my bearings.

I focus on my menu: ratatouille, coq a vin, cassoulet, salade niçoise. But my mind quickly wanders. I think of Hunter's lips, the way they molded to fit mine. Despite his clear trepidation, the kiss betrayed none of it. For the briefest of moments, his palm rested on my chest. Surely, he could feel my heartbeat, the way it skipped when my breath caught in my throat. Then, I think of Hunter's eyes when he saw us in the alley behind Ebb and Flow. It was as though I punched him, my knuckles making contact just under his chin and driving his head up and back. *Had James done it on purpose?*

Of course he did.

I shake my head. It's as though he knew I confessed my feelings. Had he been lingering on the sidewalk, lighting cigarette after cigarette? *Once more*, I'd said. In a way, James was giving it to me. He may as well have threatened the both of us. *This is the last time you'll* ever *see each other.*

Luka is talking animatedly. "I found a surfboard in Ama's house and met some kids my age on the beach. They taught me to ride it on my belly, and I nearly stood up. But then I fell and inhaled what felt like a bucket of water." He talks with his hands as if composing a song only he can hear.

James laughs. When the mustachioed waiter arrives, he takes it upon himself to order a bottle of 2017 Patient Cottat Anciennes Vignes Sancerre. He preens when the waiter deadpans, "An excellent choice, Sir."

Leigh snorts, flicking her long hair over her shoulder. "You're becoming more and more unbearable as you get older, Jay. We grew up in fucking Montana, not the South of France."

"This wine is from Central France," James replies coolly. Pretentious prick. I roll my eyes, not bothering to hide it from him. He shoots me a caustic look.

"Why can't you be more like Angus?" Leigh says. "He knows where he came from." It's a jab at me more so than James. In her eyes, I abandoned her twin in his moment of greatest weakness. *It could have happened to any of us,* she had said one night, during our trip cross-country, her bare feet on the dashboard. James and Luka had been asleep in the backseat, both snoring softly. *It could have been me—or you. No,* I had said, my eyes on the road. *I would never.* Leigh had looked at me then, her eyes forlorn. *Are you sure?*

The wine arrives and the waiter pops the cork with a flourish, a thin trickle of water vapor escaping. "Are you ready to order?" the waiter asks as he pours four glasses of the golden vino.

I order a pork tenderloin with crab cakes, though I have no appetite. I gulp my wine as soon as my glass is full, ignoring James' insistence that we smell, swish, and spit like real connoisseurs. I am haunted by Hunter's face, the fear etched therein when he saw James; the dejection when he saw James' arm slung around my shoulders.

"So," James drawls when the waiter heads back to the kitchen. "Will you really abandon your own kind for a *human*, Gus?"

I put down my empty glass, reaching for the bottle to refill it. I don't know whether to lie or tell the truth. James is dangerous now—rabid even. He still has the ghost of Nedry's essence in his belly, urging him to *hunt more, kill more, eat more*. I undoubtedly know him. I've delved inside his nooks and crannies, but what I know above all else is that he is incalculable. It's a tossup whether he will bide his time or act, and, either way, my heart will be the casualty. Hunter will surely be caught in the crossfire.

"No," I reply breezily. "I just wanted to see what it was like, is all."

"And how was it?" Luka asks, curious. He sips his wine, wrinkling his nose. He despises wine, but James is too self-absorbed to notice. *I can never taste the fruity tones or whatever*, he says. *It just tastes fucking awful.*

I shrug. Thankfully, the waiter arrives with steaming platters balanced on his arms. When he places my meal before me, I cut a bite of flaky crab cake with the side of my fork. It's too hot, but I pop it into my mouth, wincing as my tongue and the roof of my mouth is scalded. If I have my mouth full, I don't have to answer the question. In truth, the only words I can think of to describe the kiss are positive. It did make me feel guilty, but only in the way a sumptuous dessert makes one feel guilty.

James tips an oyster into his mouth, slurping the buttery mollusk with the same gusto with which he'd consumed the slippery entrails of the doe. When he places the empty shell back onto his plate, he turns his attention back to me. "Oh yes, Gus. Tell us about the human. What's his name again?"

"Hunter," I mumble. James rests his elbows on the table, his chin on his palm. I want to tell him he has shitty table manners. "It was no big deal. We kissed *once.*"

"That's why you smell like him," James replies. I try very hard not to look at the A tattooed on James' ring finger. The apex of the 'A' points at me like an arrow. I half-expect it to impale my chest wall, splitting me in two. "You smelled like arousal, too."

"I did not," I huff.

James laughs hollowly. "I'm not fucking stupid, Gus."

"Maybe it was because my ex-husband was basically lapping at my neck," I reply.

◆ ◆ ◆

We meander down Bird's Nest, toward Ama's bungalow. My toes catch in the gravel and I trip. We are all very drunk. The four of us drank several bottles of wine, then went across the street to Schooners for a round of Long Island iced teas. Leigh laughs, grasping my arm and hauling me up. Her heels dangle from a crooked finger, her bare feet far more nimble than mine. James is so sloshed that he's forgiven me, or simply forgotten my supposed transgressions. Or so I think.

Luka hurries into the long sea grass to vomit and we all pause to wait for him. James sidles up beside me, resting his chin on my shoulder. "It was really nothing?" he asks. "The *thing* with the human?" His breath is hot and steeped in rum.

"Yeah," I reply, surprised by the steadiness of my voice. "It was nothing."

"Good." James' arms encircle my waist, and he nuzzles my neck. He knows how much I love having my neck nuzzled, kissed, *bitten*. It's why he did it in front of Hunter. He knew it would make my heart skip a beat, make my breath hitch. A fresh wave of agitation laps against my stomach and I scowl at him. He simply smiles.

"Can we get moving?" Leigh whines, dancing from foot to foot. "I have to pee *so bad.*"

Luka emerges as if on cue, looking wan. "I just wasted all that money you spent on dinner," he says mournfully. "The coq a vin…"

"Come on, pup," Leigh says, grabbing his hand. "Let's get you inside." They trot ahead, and, soon enough, it seems as though Luka forgets his upset stomach. They laugh together, playfully pushing one another into the shallow ditches flanking the lane. "I just stepped in something *wet*," Leigh shrieks. When they barge into the bungalow, yelling greetings to Ama, James' arms tighten around me.

"You're telling me the truth, right?" he asks, the edge in his voice cutting me like a knife.

I shouldn't have had so much to drink; my tongue feels loose, and I feel unsteady. His arms tighten around me, and his hot breath wets the back of my neck. I turn in his arms, resting a palm against his bearded cheek. "Of course, I am."

When he kisses me, I pretend it's Hunter.

Chapter Eleven
(HUNTER)

———◁◆▷———

I stand in the storeroom of Ebb and Flow, shaking violently, clutching the stinking bag of garbage I had forgotten to toss into the dumpster. I wait until the sounds of the foursome fade away before cracking the door open and peering down the alley toward Jefferson Court. They had been heading that way. Thankfully, there's no sign of them now.

Seeing James was a kick to the knees. It's the first time I've seen him in the light of day, without fire-light contorting his features. It strikes me how normal he looks. If I passed him in the street, I would have never given him a second glance. *Well,* I concede, *he may have gotten a double take.* He's handsome, his salt-and-pepper hair slicked back, save for one errant strand resting upon his high forehead. His demeanor is self-assured, and it is apparent he is accustomed to getting whatever he likes, whenever he likes. His tattoos are colorful and crawl up his arms, adorn his throat.

It's getting late. I closed the cafe early, hoping to spend an hour or two at the fair. It's purely for nostalgia's sake; the fair was where I kissed a girl for the first time. And it was where I kissed a boy for the first time, too. But now, I just want to go home. I quickly gather my things from one of the beat-up lockers—wallet, keys, phone—and hang up my apron.

My phone vibrates in my back pocket as I walk into the cafe proper, and I nearly jump out of my skin. For the briefest of moments, I hope it's Angus. It's not.

[Geoff: Can we talk?].

[Hunter: Hey, that...]

Then, I pause. Part of me desperately wants him to come over tonight. I feel off-kilter, and he is cozy like an old hoodie. But I don't know if it's necessarily fair to him. I kissed another man just hours ago.

I erase what I've written and start over.

[Hunter: Not tonight.]

[Geoff: Please.]

The text comes in within seconds as if he knew I'd balk at the idea.

[Geoff: It can't wait. Meet at the Ferris wheel?]

I sigh, putting my phone back into my pocket so that I can lock the cafe door behind myself. If he didn't sound so desperate, I think I would just walk home and pretend my battery suddenly died. *Sorry, I forgot to charge my phone.*

[Hunter: Sure. Buy me a funnel cake?]

An ellipses appears on the screen, bobbing as he types.

[Geoff: I already bought it.]

And then, a photo of said funnel cake, nearly spilling over the edges of a flimsy paper plate. He knows me well. It's my favorite fair fare. I can't help but smile and head toward the pier, the twinkling lights at the apex of the Ferris wheel my lighthouse.

I find Geoff standing at the base of the Ferris wheel, the funnel cake in hand. He is wearing a crimson flannel button-down, the sleeves rolled up to his elbows. His glasses slip down his nose and his nostrils flare in annoyance as he pushes them back up. But when he sees me, his face brightens.

Geoff grins. "Hey," he calls, beckoning me with his free hand. "You came!"

"I can never turn down a free funnel cake," I reply, taking the warm dessert from his hands. I inhale, the smell of crispy dough and sugar filling my nostrils. It's a smell that is as homey as Geoff's spicy cologne or fresh, ground coffee beans.

"I know," he replies warmly. "Let's find a place to sit." His palm alights on the small of my back as he guides me through the crowd, toward a herd of picnic tables. Most are occupied, but we find a space on a bench, politely greeting our tablemates. Geoff and I have to sit so close our hips touch. "I wanted to talk to you," he says without preamble. "About us."

"Oh," I say, my stomach sinking. I pull a piece of coiled funnel cake off of the rest, stuffing it into my mouth. Maybe he won't expect me to talk if my mouth is full. The funnel cake is still piping hot and I wince as I swallow.

"I've been thinking a lot about it, and I want to try again. If you'll let me. I want to get married."

"I want to get married," I say. The velvet ring box sits on the patio table between us, the lid open. Inside, a circle of silver gleams, the light of the sunset making

it appear iridescent. Geoff's face—pinched, pale—emphasizes his discomfort at the idea. "It's been six years," I continue. I don't quite sound like myself. My voice wavers, thin and reedy.

"I don't want to ruin a good thing," Geoff replies slowly. "You know I don't want to get married. You knew that from the beginning," But we were twenty-five then; immature, interested in sex moreso than anything else. Neither of us intended for anything long-term. We didn't plan for six years. I was stupid to think he would change his mind. Geoff reaches toward the ring box and closes the box with his finger. "I'm sorry." A week later, he moved out and I tucked the engagement ring into a box in the back of my closet, nestled amidst clothes I meant to donate months ago.

"You do?" I push the plate away. I've lost my appetite.

Geoff touches my hand. "Being without you has been terrible. These last few weeks—sharing our bed again—made me realize how desperately I want our life back." He's speaking quickly, the words tumbling out into a heap. It's as though he memorized this, weighing each word. "I've been miserable."

I've been miserable too.

"And," he says. "If marriage is what gets you back, then let's get married."

You know I don't want to get married, he'd said. Could he really have had a change of heart? Or is he as desperate as he says? If it's the latter, then he will resent me forever. That much is clear. I remember his hunched shoulders the day after my proposal, the way he shrugged me off when I tried to embrace him. He was so angry at me.

"I—" This is what I'd wanted. Back then, I'd wanted this so badly that my stomach ached. After he said no, I walked out to the beach barefoot and sobbed, the breaking waves drowning out the noise. I sat out there for hours, wishing he would rush out and fall to his knees beside me. The Geoff in my fantasy would tell me he made an enormous mistake, and that he wanted the same fairytale I did. But when I finally returned home, he was sound asleep in our bed.

Geoff squeezes my hand, lifting it to his mouth to kiss my knuckles. "Please say yes," he whispers.

"Are you proposing?" I ask, my mouth dry.

Geoff fishes in his chest pocket and produces a simple ring, made of hammered gold. "I know this isn't much, but it's all I could get on short notice. Marry me, Hunt."

The strangers at the table are watching now, waiting with bated breath for my answer. A teenage girl pulls out her phone, aiming the lens at me.

I abruptly rise, awkwardly stepping backward over the bench. "I can't do this here." I hesitate when I see his face, his mouth slack, and his eyes wide. He expected me to fall all over him, like a princess who waited ages for her prince to rescue her. But I turn away, speed-walking down the pier. I find myself oscillating between abject sadness and anger.

[Geoff: Hunt, please. I love you.]
Then...
[Geoff: I'm sorry I did this in public.]

He thinks I'm embarrassed, not that I intended to say no. Or had I already said no, purely by walking away? Bird's Nest is dark when I reach it, the few streetlights offering dim pools of light. When I reach the bungalow, I mount the stairs, stepping around the crab traps and the bicycle missing its wheel. The lights are out.

I knock and am relieved when he answers. Angus is half-naked, only wearing a pair of tight boxer briefs. I'm not sure what I would have done if one of the others had answered. I'm not thinking clearly; even the possibility of being face-to-face with James doesn't seem all that frightening.

Angus looks at me, bleary-eyed. Clearly, he had been asleep, "Hunter?" he says in surprise. He hurriedly steps onto the porch, firmly shutting the door behind him. "What are you doing here?" he whispers.

"Can we talk?" I ask in a rush. I am too loud, and he winces. I think of James and the others, all of whom are undoubtedly inside, and I clap my hand over my mouth.

Angus glances back at the house, wearily. "Come with me," he urges, taking my hand and leading me around the side of the bungalow, toward the beach. We walk in silence, both huffing as we trudge through the thick sand. We find a spot bereft of footprints and sit together. I pull my knees up to my chest, wrapping my arms around my knobby knees. Angus stretches his legs out before him, leaning back on his elbows. "Are you okay?" he asks, giving me a sidelong look. "You look like shit."

I can't help but laugh, the sound akin to a croupy cough. "No," I admit. "I'm not okay."

"Is it because of what happened earlier?" For a moment, I don't know what he's referring to. It has been a long, *long* night. James' bravado—and the inherent threat—in the alleyway seems like eons ago.

"Geoff proposed," I mumble, looking out at the vast expanse of the ocean.

In the dark, it looks like tar. My phone vibrates in my pocket and I ignore it. I can't bear to read Geoff's words. It will just be more groveling, pleading, and, knowing Geoff, soon both would be replaced by something akin to despondency. He is prone to collapse into himself like a neutron star, scribbling in a sketchbook with thick swathes of graphite until all of his thoughts are compartmentalized therein. He keeps those moleskins private, guarding them like a dragon languishing on a nest of gold. I saw one page in passing: a sketch of my profile, my eyes dark chasms, my frown so deep it gave me jowls.

Angus sits up. "Oh," he replies, his tone unreadable. "So, you're getting married."

"No." I shake my head.

"Why not?" I try very hard not to look at Angus' body. His thighs are thick and toned. His abdomen seems etched from marble, a trail of dark, wiry hair leading to the waistband of his underwear. I try doubly hard not to look at the shape of him beneath the stretchy cloth of his dark-colored briefs.

Stop it, I tell myself, *you're not in your right mind.*

"I don't think he really wanted to marry me," I say slowly. The words taste bitter and I spit them out. "He just wanted to appease me so he could move back in."

"I'm sorry," Angus says, reaching for my hand and giving it a squeeze. "I'm really sorry."

"I don't know why I came here." I meet his eyes, struck, as usual, by their blueness. They remind me of the ocean in a child's drawing: aggressively cyan, a shaky cyclone of amorphous color.

He tentatively reaches for me, stroking my cheekbone with the rough pad of his thumb. There's a brief moment where his thumb swipes against my upper lip and I can't help but let out a soft groan. It embarrasses me, and I cast my eyes downward. Slowly, excruciatingly so, Angus tips my chin so that he can lean close, his lips glancing against mine. Our breath intermingles and I realize he's waiting for me to speak, to act, to do something.

"Kiss me," I murmur, tentatively cupping the back of his neck. His skin is warm, and my fingers tangle in his long hair. "Angus, I really want you to kiss me." Gently, Angus untangles my limbs so that he can lay me back in the sand, his lips pressing against mine. He tastes like spearmint and he smells good: musky, ostensibly masculine, with a hint of tangerine.

For a moment, I think of Geoff sitting at that picnic table, the ring held between his thumb and forefinger. Behind him, the Ferris wheel slowly rotates, a brilliant halo for a less-than saintly paragon. But I realize he's not looking at me, not really. He's looking at the ring, and I know what he's thinking. *This is the shackle I'll wear to go back to normal.* Angus' fingertips trail down my abdomen, and Geoff dissipates like smoke. "You taste so good," Angus murmurs into my mouth, his tongue lapping against mine.

I am suddenly cognizant of Angus' hardness against my thigh. When he shifts his weight to straddle my hips, I feel scared. This is how James held me down, his hot saliva dripping onto my cheeks where it mixed with my tears. Angus could do the same, if he so wanted. "Wait—"

Angus freezes, looking down at me. "Do you want me to stop?" His voice is gentle, peppered with concern.

"I—" I press my lips together. *I don't want to stop.* "I just—sorry—Angus, James held me down like this."

"Oh," he murmurs, sliding off me. "I wasn't thinking." He sits cross-legged in the sand, his hands in his lap. His cock stands at attention, but Angus isn't angry at me. Or he's very good at hiding his emotions. Geoff would have pouted, cajoled, pushed and pushed. "How about we go to your place, have a midnight snack, and talk?" he suggests.

"Okay," I say. Angus clambers to his feet, brushing sand off of his thighs. He pulls me up, and, before we go, he kisses me again.

♦ ♦ ♦

Scree! The teapot startles me, and I jump in my chair. Angus removes it from the burner, pouring the boiling water into my French press. The coffee grounds incorporate with the water, the dark motes swirling. "I don't know how you can drink coffee right now," I remark.

Angus laughs. "I like coffee. Maybe that's why I like you." He winks at me, and my stomach flip-flops. *I like him too.*

When we arrived at my bungalow, we fell into an easy rhythm. Angus greeted Ghost, scratching him under the chin. He insisted I sit while he opened and closed cabinets, searching for something tasty. There wasn't much, save for a half-eaten bag of pita crisps and hummus. I don't take any of the proffered snack, but Angus is nonplussed. He simply pops a crisp with a heaping helping of hummus into his mouth before he starts the coffee.

It's strange, having a half-naked man in my kitchen. In the fluorescent lighting, I can see every curve and valley of him. I am particularly distracted by his ass, the tight spandex leaving little to the imagination. While waiting a few moments for the coffee to brew, Angus searches for a coffee mug.

"Top shelf to the left," I say, distracted. I have an expansive mug collection. It's the most banal thing about me. *Of course* the barista has a lot of coffee accoutrements in his home. Thus, the French press, and the coffee grinder, and the *perfect* mugs for practicing latte art. And and and.

Angus selects a mug with a pink, red, and purple gradient. It's one of Geoff's creations, and I inwardly wince. I can't seem to escape him. Again, thoughts of that ring crowd my thoughts. "Are you sure you don't want any?" Angus asks. He presses the plunger into the French press in one smooth motion, pouring the coffee into his mug.

"No, no," I reply, waving him off. My phone vibrates and I look at it without thinking.

[Geoff: I'm coming over. I know you're still awake.]

"*Fuck,*" I groan.

Angus leans back against the counter, sipping his coffee. "What's up?"

"It's Geoff. He says he's coming over."

"Do you want him to?" Angus' face is impassive, his tone curious more so than anything else.

"No, no. I don't want you to go. Maybe if I don't text, and don't answer the door, he'll go away." I know that's not true. Geoff will camp out on the porch if need be. He is stubborn, and I'm sure a little indignant. I scroll through the texts he sent since I started to ignore them:

[Geoff: You wanted this.]

[Geoff: Maybe I did it wrong. But, what the *fuck?*]

[Geoff: Are you ghosting me now?]

[Geoff: Please.]

[Geoff: Sometimes I think you *try* to be unhappy.]

A lot *indignant*. Angus gently takes the phone from my hand, putting it face down on the tabletop without so much as a glance. "Your jaw is so tight I worry you'll snap your molars," he jokes. He urges me to my feet, a hand on the small of my back pulling me close. Our hips fit together like puzzle pieces. "Shall I answer the door naked?" he purrs.

Heat pours into my groin. "Angus—" He is far taller than me, forcing me up onto my tiptoes to press my lips against his. I have been so bold with him. It's

127

beyond reason. After all, there's a part of him that is terrifying, otherworldly. But I can't help it. I want him so, so badly. When he looks at me, I ignite; I'm a pyre, a torch, a matchstick.

I'm a *bonfire* on a beach.

Angus deepens the kiss, his big hands squeezing my ass. Then, he lifts me off of my feet, setting me atop the kitchen table. He steps between my legs, leaning close so that he can kiss me hard. My fingers tangle in his long hair.

Suddenly, he nips my lip, hard, and I jerk away from him. I gently probe my lip with my fingers and examine the streak of pinkish blood. "Oh," I say.

"I'm sorry." Angus says. He catches my wrist in his big hand, surveying the blood on my fingertip. His nostrils flare. "I'm sorry," he repeats, licking his lips with the tip of his pink tongue. "Let me clean that up." He leaves me perched atop the tabletop, searching my drawers for a washcloth. Finding one, he wets it under the faucet. His eyes, veritable riptides, meet mine as he dabs my lower lip, tilting my chin this way and that.

"It's—" I'm not sure what to say. A trickle of fear edges down my spine. I almost forgot what he was. I can't help but to think of him from the night of the bonfire: his teeth, keen and impossibly sharp; his eyes, still blue but like the deepest depths of the Mariana Trench; his body, rangy with ropes of muscle and adorned with white fur. In the firelight, he looked like liquid mercury. "It's just—"

"Hunter." Angus tilts my chin so that he can look into my eyes. "I would never hurt you. You never have to see me *like that* if you don't want to." I am secretly relieved. "I'm sorry this happened," he continues. "I just... want you so badly."

There's a knock on the front door. *Geoff.* "Fuck," I groan. I can almost see him out there, the ring burning a hole in his pocket.

"Don't answer it," Angus croons, softly kissing my lips. "Stay here with me." My phone vibrates on the tabletop. I begin to reach for it, but Angus laces his fingers with mine. The doorbell rings, then rings again. "Or, better yet, I can answer it." He takes my hand, showing me that his cock is stiff and straining against his underwear. I gasp.

"I'll pretend like I'm not home," I murmur. I run my palms over Angus' broad back, the knobs of his spine protruding. I quickly forget the throbbing in my lip.

"We'd better hide then," Angus says, flashing me a cheeky smile. "Where shall we go?"

"D'ya wanna see my bedroom?" I ask, brazen. "It's in the back of the house."

"I would love to." I slide off of the table, sucking my teeth when our hips butt together. I take his hand, leading him down the hall.

Behind me, the doorbell rings again. My bedroom is relatively small, made up of a king-sized bed and a squat dresser. The door to the back deck is ajar, and hot air ruffles my hair. A large canvas leans against the wall, turned backward to reveal the roughhewn pine of the frame. I couldn't bear to look at that painting anymore. It's a beach scene, innocuous. But Geoff painted it for me when we first moved in together. It was a promise, or so I had thought.

Angus' lips press against the spot behind my ear. "You're beautiful," he whispers. His arms encircle my waist, pulling me back against his warmth. At his touch, my cock tents my jeans. *God*. From behind, he loosens my belt, unbuttoning my jeans with little effort. "What do you want, Hunter?" he asks.

No one has ever asked me that before. Geoff always assumed I wanted exactly what he did. He would bury his face in the curve of my neck, gasping and groaning. *Oh yeah, oh yeah, you like that?* He wasn't really asking. "I want..." I swallow. "I want to go slow. I want to look at you."

The doorbell rings again, but it sounds very far away, inconsequential. Angus' hands slip under the hem of my shirt, running up my abdomen. "I can do that," he murmurs. I turn in his arms, looking up at his face. His jaw tightens and loosens. I want to know what he's thinking, but I feel suddenly bashful. He tilts his head to kiss me, his lips as soft as rose petals. "Tell me what to do," he whispers.

I'm scared to utter my desires aloud. But he's waiting, his face inches from mine, his thumb making concentric circles along my jawline. "I want you to take your clothes off," I finally say. My voice is strangely steady, though I feel imbued with a kinetic energy. I tremble.

Meeting my eyes, Angus pulls down his boxer briefs, stepping out of them. His turgid cock is impossibly hard, the head shiny with precum. I touch it, first tentative, then with gusto. He is thick and fills my hand.

When I start to stroke him, he groans under his breath. "Hunter." His eyelids flutter closed, and he bites at his lip, the flesh blanching. "That feels so good." I stroke him more quickly, delighting at the way my touch makes his eyebrows knit together. "So good," he repeats. Suddenly his hand covers mine, stopping me.

"Let me take these off," Angus growls, tugging at the belt loops of my jeans. My cock strains against my underwear, a moist dot of precum on the fabric. I am desperate for him to touch me, stroke me, fuck me. The doorbell rings thrice in quick succession. Geoff is getting impatient. Slowly, excruciatingly slowly, Angus kneels, pulling down my underwear and kissing the soft flesh of my inner thighs. "Do you want this?" Angus asks, his hot breath at the base of my cock.

"Yeah," I groan, reaching for and fisting his hair. "Angus, please—" His mouth descends upon me, and his tongue swirls around my swollen head. "That feels so good," I groan, urging him onward with my hand. As his head bobs up and down on my cock, I pant like a dog in summertime. The doorbell rings in a quick, agitated staccato: *ring, ring, ringringring!*

Angus lifts his head, surveying me as he works my cock with his firm hand. "He really is persistent, isn't he?"

"Uh huh," I manage. Right now, I don't care about Geoff. I urge Angus to his feet. I want to make him feel good, too. Tentative, I sink onto my knees before him. When I take him into my mouth, my lips stretched to accommodate him, a guttural moan escapes his parted lips. He rocks his hips. I cup his cool balls in my palm, giving them a gentle squeeze.

"You feel so good," he says, breathless. The door-bell rings again, the note sustained. I can see Geoff in my mind's eye holding the button down, the keening sound a poor substitute for his voice. I wonder if he realizes that his desperation isn't helping his cause. Instead, it makes him appear entitled. *I deserve you.* I close my eyes, trying very hard to focus on the here-and-now, and the man who unabashedly wants me. No stipulations.

Suddenly, Angus urges me to my feet, kissing me hard. "I want to be inside of you," he says. "Do you want that?"

"Yeah," I reply huskily.

"Hands and knees." Angus' voice is firm, but kind. He gestured to the bed. When I am positioned, he kisses the small of my back. "Beautiful," he whis-pers, sliding his cock up and down the crack of my ass. Then, he presses the head against my tight hole, gasping as he slowly slips inside.

I fist the comforter with both hands as he fills me. Then, he thrusts in and out of me, first slowly, then with vigor. I pant, my breath synchronous with his movements. *Pant, pant, pant. Yes, yes, yes!*

His hand rests on my shoulder, his nails making half-moons in my flesh. I'm getting close, and he is too. His thrusts become jerky; his grip tightens on my hips.

"Angus—" I whimper.

"I'm gonna cum, baby," he howls, abruptly pulling out. Thick ropes of cum adorn my back as his orgasm ripples through his body. "Oh god." His hands grip the twin globes of my ass, and he gently pulls them apart, his tongue probing my asshole. It's a feeling I've never experienced before. Geoff was very much adverse to anything more taboo than a blowjob. While Angus circles my puckered hole with his tongue, he pumps my cock with enthusiasm.

Then, my own orgasm washes over me like a tidal wave. I cry out and collapse onto the mattress, spent.

The doorbell stops.

Angus presses his lips against my shoulder. "I'm sorry," he mumbles, his voice full of emotion. "I should have been more careful." He's talking about the indentations left by his fingernails.

"It's okay," I assure him. "I liked it."

"I'll be more careful," he says, "next time."

"There'll be a next time?" I ask, propping myself up on my elbow to look down at him.

His long hair is mussed, a tangle atop his head. The scars on his cheeks seem to stretch in the darkness, disappearing into his hairline. It's a trick of the light, nothing more. But it reminds me of the way James' skull freakishly elongated.

Will I always think of James when I see Angus' handsome face?

CHAPTER TWELVE
(JAMES)

———◁◆▷———

*H*e's lying to me. When we share a kiss after Le Petite Crique, his eyes go vacant. The light goes out. No one's home. When we crawl into bed each night, forced together by necessity, he rolls away, pulling the scratchy blankets over his naked shoulders. *It was nothing.* Right.

When he doesn't come home, I follow his scent down to the beach. He isn't there anymore, but I can see the hollow made by his body, the imprints of his palms. I catch another scent there, the same one that I washed off of myself after the bonfire. *Eau de Scum*—Hunter Bailey. I track them along the shoreline, following their tracks. I can almost see them in my mind's eye. Angus likes to hold hands. Surely, he'll be running his thumb over Hunter's in slow concentric circles. It's a habit, but it's also an implicit promise. *I'll make you feel so good,* it says. He used to do it to me in bars while he spoke to our friends. Then, he would lead me into the alley and unbutton my jeans. He really can be insatiable.

They walk back toward Bird's Nest, their footsteps forming deep impressions in the thick sand as I slog behind them. When I near a bungalow—similar, if not identical, to Ama's—my nostrils are full of them. I slowly approach the back porch, mounting the steps. There's a screen door, swinging a bit on its hinges when the salt air laps against it just right. The room beyond it is pitch-black, but I can hear breathing. Suddenly, a phone inside buzzes and the screen illuminates on a bedside table. It's dim, but, for a second, I can see them. They are asleep, curled together like puppies.

The sound of the phone wakes Hunter, and he slowly sits up in bed. He reaches around Angus' naked shoulder to retrieve the phone, careful not to wake him. His face awash in the phone's glow, I can almost see what Angus sees in him. His cheekbones are high, his jaw squarish and lightly stubbled. His green eyes look nearly grey. He mumbles to himself, the words indecipherable.

"Come back to bed," Angus murmurs.

"He hasn't stopped texting," Hunter says, unable to wrench his eyes away from the screen. "They're still coming in. Look at this one. He calls me a 'cunt.'"

Angus takes the phone from Hunter's hand, hiding it behind his back. "Come back to bed," he insists. When the phone's screen dims, it's far more difficult to see them. I can only see vague shapes that sink into and out of the shadows when I blink. The two bodies melt together and soon, their breath quickens. "Hunter," Angus breathes.

He has said my name hundreds—*thousands*—of times, but I haven't heard him say it like that. It's as though Hunter is a sumptuous meal with a decanter of wine. It's as though he's the type of dish one must admire, smell, gently prod with the edge of one's fork.

My skin prickles. But despite myself, I turn away from the sounds of lovemaking. *Be patient*, I tell myself. Angus will ruin this relationship by himself, and I'll be here to pick up the pieces.

But I can quicken the process, can't I?

CHAPTER THIRTEEN
(ANGUS)

———◁◆▷———

I sit outside Ebb and Flow, the sun warming my naked shoulders. I borrowed a tank top and board shorts from Hunter's closet. They are too tight.

"God, you can see *everything*," Hunter had groaned. "Come back to bed."

The ice in my coffee rattles as I take a sip. If I look through the large picture window, I can just make out Hunter behind the counter, busily taking orders and making drinks. Every once in a while, he looks up and catches my eye, grinning.

I spent the night after our lovemaking curled around his small body, breathing in the smell of his skin. He couldn't possibly know this—or understand it—but his pheromones are intoxicating to me. The smell of his sweat makes me heady, and I must resist the urge to drag the flat of my tongue up his neck. I very nearly surrendered to the impulse. I expect he would taste so good. Fucking him was a test of discipline. There was a part of me—a terrifying part—that wanted to sink my teeth into him. When I was inside of him, he turned his head to look at me with one rolling eye, and I thought of a terrified hare.

When we wake, we idle in bed, speaking in whispers. I tell him about my mother, who died in a car accident; my father, who may as well have died, too. Hunter grasps my hand in the dark, and says "my mom, too." His dad, he says, lives in the Midwest, spending his retirement solving sudoku and chatting up all of the eligible over-fifty-fives at the Elks club. My dad, I reply, could be anywhere—he could be anyone, really. We haven't spoken in thirteen years, and his face has been distorted by time. Memory is a fickle thing. "I'm so sorry," Hunter says, nuzzling my neck. "Really, Angus, that's horrible."

I don't want to talk anymore, so I kiss his shoulder, running my hands down his back. His muscles jump under my palms, and I pull him close. Hunter mewls.

"I think—" I breathe, into his ear, dragging the very tip of my tongue along his velvety earlobe.

"Hmm?"

"—I think I would like us to stop talking," I finish. I roll onto my back, pulling him astride my hips. We are still naked, and I watch as his cock grows firm between our bodies. I long to kiss the intumescent head, but I have other plans. "I think that I would like you to be inside of me."

"Really?" Hunter rests his palms on my chest, making my nipples peak with his thumbs.

I encircle the back of his neck with my hand, pulling him close. The raised, scarred skin there reminds me of James, and a lava flow of anger rolls through my belly.

Hunter lets me pull him close, and he reaches between us to adjust his cock so that it probes the puckered flesh of my asshole. I take his hand, drawing his fingers into my mouth until they are slick with saliva.

Then, he uses that hand to jerk at his turgid cock, his movements spasmodic. "You want this?" he growls, flexing so that his hips grind against my ass.

He's so cute.

"Oh yeah," I reply, flashing him a smile. Hunter looks so serious. His brow is tensed, and his jaw is all right angles. Excruciatingly slowly, he presses into me, and I pull my knees up to accommodate him. *Oh god!*

"You feel so good," he gasps, gripping my hips tight and burying himself to the hilt. He feels good, too. "I'm already so close."

Our mouths crash together, and his tongue slithers into my mouth. He rests his palms on either side of my head, his forearms bulging as he thrusts again, and again, and again. When Hunter finally cums, I drag my tongue over his chest, concealing the gesture behind a smattering of kisses. He tastes briny from sweat, and it reminds me of sucking oysters from their shells. I am unprepared for the hunger pang that follows.

When Hunter's soft mouth wraps around my cock, I try very hard to push the feeling away.

We walk together to the cafe at dawn, holding hands, and he blushes like a schoolgirl whenever we pass by someone exercising, opening their shuttered stores, or coming home from a night out, clothes rumpled and hair mussed. It's cute. I watch curiously as he opens the cafe while cupping a mug of hot coffee between my palms.

Two women enter a few moments after I get settled, and survey me curiously. The younger of the two leans close to Hunter and says, "you didn't fuck in here, did you?"

"Renee!" he hisses, shooting me an embarrassed look.

The other woman glares at me, her mouth a thin line. I am struck by how similar she looks to Hunter. They both have the same eyes, though hers are far darker. "Really, Hunt?" she says, exasperated, returning her attention to my lover.

This was when I chose to sit outside, slipping out when the woman hustled Hunter into the backroom.

After the cafe opens, Hunter slips out to bring me a cheese danish and my favorite: an iced coffee, creamy with soy milk. "Sorry," he mumbles. "That was my sister, Candy." His hand alights upon my shoulder for a moment.

"She doesn't like me," I observe.

"It's not that," Hunter says with a sigh. "She lives with Geoff. I'm sure he was *upset* when he arrived home. Then, seeing you here, she put two and two together."

What a complicated situation. It must be so terrible for Hunter, having to contend with so many peoples' feelings about his relationship—or lack thereof. I don't want to make any assumptions about him and me. My side of this is complicated too. *I'm* complicated.

"I've got to get back inside," Hunter says, squeezing my shoulder.

I pick at the cheese danish on my plate. I am ravenous, but I want to savor it. The cream cheese is soft and silky, dissolving on my tongue. The pastry is flakey and, try as I might, I can't quite contain the crumbs. The plate—green, triangular etchings on the rim—is a mess. I press my forefinger against the cool surface and pop the morsels into my mouth. I find myself people watching; Main Street is highly trafficked, and people walk into and out of stores, like ants carrying food back to their colonies. There's a sale at the antique store across the street, and most of the patrons emerge with dusty trinkets: a Tiffany lamp, a lawn jockey with a chip in its facade, a violin case with faded stickers plastered on its side.

Leigh emerges from the store, a cardboard box under her arm. I hope she doesn't spot me, but our eyes meet. "Angus!" she calls, looking left and right before trotting across the street. Without being invited, she drops into the chair across from me, setting her package at her feet. "You're up early," she observes.

I grunt in response, hoping she will take the hint and go away. The last thing I want is for her to report back to her brother; she has a big mouth.

"Someone is acting shitty this morning," she huffs. "I'm getting a coffee. Watch my stuff." She rises and heads inside. I watch her approach the counter, and Hunter's face grow pale when he sees her. Setting his jaw, he takes her order. She glances through the window at me before paying and taking her cup of drip coffee. Black. When she emerges, her excitement is palpable. "Oh my *god*," she squeaks. "He *smells* like you. What were you *up to* last night?"

I give her a withering look. "What does it matter?"

"Angus," she snorts, "of course it matters. He's a human. Not only that, he's also the human my brother tried to *murder*."

"I seem to remember a certain she-wolf who helped with that," I say dryly.

She waves the accusation away. "You're being just as impulsive and stupid as James."

The laughter bursts from my chest. It is humorless, a bark. "How so?" I take a long drag of my coffee, the coolness quelling the angry heat bubbling to the surface. *How dare she compare my behavior to his!*

Leigh leans close. "You're going to expose us. Where would we go then?"

"Hunter wouldn't do that," I reply, indignant. "There's no fucking way."

"Yeah, and James thinks he's invincible. You deserved each other." She reaches across the table and takes what remains of my danish, popping it into her mouth. "He will be *pissed* when he finds out about this."

"We aren't together anymore," I remind her.

"Yeah," she snorts. "Don't act like my brother wasn't all over you last night."

I think of James on the walk home from the bar, the heat of his breath on my neck. His wanting was palpable, and I didn't spurn him. Nor did I encourage him.

"Listen," I begin. "I don't give a fuck about what your brother feels or thinks. He's lucky I didn't kill him in Portland, and that I *let* him come here with us." She scoffs, but I shush her. "Listen to your Alpha, Leigh."

Leigh winces. "I won't tell him, okay?" She takes a sip of her coffee, her eyes downcast. She may as well be showing her belly, licking at my chin. "I promise." She rises, gathering her things. "Angus, I—" She pauses, unsure. "Just be careful, okay? James is dangerous. He's different. I... don't think I know him anymore." Leigh hesitates for another moment before walking briskly away, shoulders hunched.

I finish my coffee, a pile of melting ice remaining. I want another. After all, I didn't get much sleep last night. I head inside and sidle up to the counter. When Hunter spots me, he blushes a deep crimson. "Hi," he says.

I grin at him, giving him a wink. The blush crawls down that beautiful neck. "Can I get another iced coffee? Soy."

"Of course." As he pours the coffee over ice, I admire his tapered fingers, so delicate and yet, blemished by white, raised burn scars. The perils of working with hot liquids and baking sumptuous desserts. Those beautiful fingers expertly brought me to orgasm and, later, stroked my cheek. *I'm happy*, he had said, sleepily. *I really am happy.*

When he delivers the drink to me, I grasp his wrist, giving him a gentle tug. "Let's go back to your place," I urge him. "Right now."

He laughs, shaking me off. "I wish. But tonight? I'm closing up at 9 o'clock."

"Tonight."

Suddenly, Hunter's smiling face drops away. He's looking at the window. When I turn to look, I groan.

It's James, casually standing outside, a cigarette dangling from his mouth. He gives us both a derisive wave. *Shit*.

"It's okay, Hunt," I murmur, not taking my eyes off my ex-husband.

"Is it?" Hunter's voice shakes.

"You're safe," I assure him, "with me. I promised you, remember?"

A group of teens enter the cafe (*ding-ding!*) and Hunter jumps. They crowd around the register and he is forced to turn his attention to them. His movements are stilted; it's difficult to act normally when you are being watched.

"I'll see you at nine," I tell him tersely. "Right here.

He nods.

I exit the cafe, making a beeline for James. "What the fuck are you doing here?" I ask, grabbing a fistful of his shirt and walking him backward into the alley.

James laughs. "I just came to get some coffee. I didn't expect to see you eye-fucking the barista. You really are playing with fire, Gus."

"Interesting choice of words," I snap, thinking of his bonfire ruse. "Stay away from him."

James raises his hands, palms outward. "Hey, *hey*. I didn't threaten anybody. I just think he's *beneath* you. Though—" James leans close, his nostrils flaring. "—it smells like he's already been beneath you."

"Fuck you."

He cackles. "I *wish*." He roughly cups my soft cock through my shorts. "I miss this." I push him so hard he takes several steps backward, nearly colliding with the opposite wall.

"You and me?" I snort. "We're over. And that's *your* fault."

"At least I'm not fucking a *human*. What was it like? Did he make you feel like a big, strong wolf? How big is your ego now?" James sneers.

I place my hand in the center of his chest, pinning him between myself and the wall. I want to claw his fucking face off. "I'm going to tell you this one more time. Stay away from Hunter. Or else I'll do what I should have done in Portland."

"You don't have the balls," James spits. "Let go of me."

I release him, walking toward the mouth of the alleyway. "Go home," I tell him, over my shoulder.

When I return to Main Street, I shove my hands into my pockets. I'm furious, vibrating with it. The flesh at the nape of my neck prickles, the telltale sign that precedes wolfishness. *Breathe*. My nails grow sharp, penetrating the lining of my pockets. *Breathe!*

I don't realize I've stumbled back into the cafe until I hear his voice. "Angus?" Hunter asks. "Are you okay?" His hands grip my upper arms. My muscles twang beneath his palms. *Breathe!* Hunter's eyes search mine, and I wish I could sink into those dark pools until I am weightless.

"I'm—" I manage. I close my eyes, focusing on my rattling breath. When I open my eyes, Hunter's face fills my vision. His hair is slightly mussed. He runs his hands through it whenever he's thinking; a tic he doesn't seem to notice. His brows furrow.

"Angus—" Hunter's eyes don't leave mine, even when the doorbell jingles.

I vaguely hear Candy speaking to whomever arrived, but I'm mesmerized by Hunter's face. His freckles are constellations. Overcome, I kiss him hard. Despite his apparent concern, he melts in my hands. My sharp talons become blunt crescents. The paresthesia abates. When I pull away, he is breathless, and his cheeks are rosy.

The sound of shattering glass turns our heads. Geoff glares at us, stony-faced, a coffee mug broken at his feet. "So," he spits, "this is why you've been ignoring me." Hunter stiffens beside me, his mouth gaping like a fish. He wraps his arms around his abdomen, curling into himself.

"No," he manages. "Geoff, it's not what it looks like."

I huff, raking my fingers through my hair. *It's not what it looks like.* The words are like a lance between the ribs, the point snapping therein.

"Shut the fuck up," Geoff says, teeth gritted. "I don't want to hear it. You could have at least told me 'no.' But *this*? This is so immature." He laughs hollowly. "And in front of your customers too."

I am suddenly aware of the many eyes on us. In a small, sleepy town, this will spread like wildfire. *Did you hear? How scandalous!* The woman who sits by the window every morning looks particularly aghast, her knitting in hand. She's mid-purl, and the loop is dangerously close to falling off the needle. A teen with an iPhone unabashedly records the scene. We'll be Tik Tok famous before sunset. Candy, too, is watching, the register open and a five-dollar bill in hand.

"I don't know what you expected," Hunter finally says, the words bursting from him as though they've been brewing for eons. "You proposed just to get me back. You told me over and over just two months ago that you would never get married. That the 'institution of marriage was bullshit.' You moved out."

"I didn't expect you to fuck me, and then, fuck someone else a week later," Geoff says, coolly. His eyes meet mine. "Did he tell you that?"

"Get out of here, Geoff," Hunter murmurs. "We can talk later."

Geoff snatches his five-dollar bill from Candy's hand. "I don't want to talk to you," he says as he heads toward the door in a huff. "Have a nice life."

The door slams shut behind him, causing the bell to crack against the doorframe with a resounding *biiiiiiiing blonk!* Hunter sighs, retrieving a broom from behind the counter. I stand anchored where he's left me, unsure what to do. All eyes remain on me.

"Show's over," I growl. Hunter avoids my eyes as he sweeps. "I'm leaving," I tell him gruffly.

"Wait." Hunter grasps my sleeve. "Come over tonight. Like we planned. I need to clean this all up." He gestures to the cafe in its entirety as if to say, *look at the mess I've made.* His face and neck are covered in red blooms, and his lip trembles as if he is about to cry.

"Yeah, okay." When I step outside, the heat immediately causes me to sweat. It's one of those days Virginians like to call "second summer": a blistering hot day after several cooler ones. It's a bizarre juxtaposition between the autumnal leaves and the rising temperature. It will be even hotter by noon. I walk down Main Street, planning to head to Ama's to shower and change clothes, but when I step onto the boardwalk, someone roughly grabs my arm.

It's Geoff. "Stay away from Hunter," he snarls without preamble. A sheen of sweat wets his brow, and his eyes are glassy with unfettered rage. I shake him off.

"Why would I do that?"

"I love him," Geoff snaps. "We're supposed to get married." He's indignant, like a child who just got his ball taken away. He may as well have stomped his foot and squealed for his mother.

"You have a funny way of showing it," I say with a laugh. I turn away, but he grabs me again. Before I can turn back and tell him off, he punches me in the jaw. For a moment, I just look at him, mouth agape. I can't help but laugh. He has no idea who he's fucking with. "No wonder Hunter dumped you." I laugh. I know that I'm trying to start a fight, but I can't help myself. This man stayed outside of Hunter's house, depressing the doorbell, and calling until Hunter's phone died. I try not to think about how I effectively did the same thing after the bonfire by lurking outside, but it *was* different, wasn't it? "Walk away, Geoff."

"Is that a threat?" Geoff snarls.

"You threatened me first, sweetheart." My retort makes him mad and he swings at me again. I easily step just outside of the arc of his punch. "I'm not going to fight you," I tell him coolly.

"I love him!" Geoff repeats. "You're just a fucking body keeping him warm." Then, he stomps on my kneecap with his Doc Marten boot. Something cracks, and I crumple to the ground. The pain radiates outwards, and I hiss through my teeth.

"Fuck!" Noticing an advantage, Geoff aims for my head, but I grab his foot, yanking him to the ground too. He lets out an *oomph* as he lands on his back. We tussle for a moment, but I am far stronger. I straddle his hips and curl my hands around his throat. "I'll kill you," I growl. As I tighten my grip, his mouth gapes. The color drains from his face. I'm not whether it's from fear or imminent asphyxiation. It's as though I have tunnel vision. All I see is his face, my hands; there's no room for anything else.

"Can't...breathe," he manages.

I lean close, tilting my head so that my ear is inches from his gaping mouth, listening to his labored breathing. There is something inherently powerful about this moment. It's terrifying too. All I can think about is squeezing just a tiny bit harder. If I were in wolf form, I could shatter every vertebrae in his neck. James said that the act of killing was invigorating; it felt undoubtedly right. Right now, I think that I understand. I think that I could kill Geoff without remorse. He causes Hunter pain, and all I want to do is ameliorate it.

I squeeze just a tad tighter, watching as his face grow all the more wan. "Can't..." he sputters. It really does feel good. Does he taste good, too? Saliva pools in my mouth, and I watch, fascinated, as my claws lengthen, leaving divots in his flesh. "I..." he croaks, his voice softer now.

"Hey!" a man shouts. I turn to see a balding man jogging toward us, waving a Louisville slugger. "Break it up!"

Caught, I leap to my feet. Geoff fills his lungs with air, a torrent of coughs folding him in half. I step over him and continue onward, ignoring the shouts behind me. I dimly notice a woman in a red bikini watching me, her sunglasses tipping down the bridge of her nose. Her eyebrows are shaved, only the brow bone raising in surprise.

I speed-walk down the boardwalk and break into a run when I reach Bird's Nest. When I look back, shuffling backward, I find that I am alone. No one is pursuing me. They don't need to. Geoff knows exactly who attacked him. He looked into my eyes while I squeezed the life out of him.

Chapter Fourteen
(HUNTER)

――――◁◆▷――――

A ngus will be here soon. I wash my face and reapply deodorant, wishing I had time to shower. Ghost bats at the water trickling from the faucet. When the doorbell rings, Ghost jettisons off of the counter, skittering under the bed. He's not usually so flighty.

When I open the door, I am surprised to find it's not Angus; it's Leigh. She's just come from the beach; she smells like coconut suntan lotion, and her red bikini is visible beneath a linen kimono. Before I can shut the door in her face, she sashays past me, flopping down onto the couch as if she owns the place.

"Can I help you?" I ask through gritted teeth. I'm angry at the intrusion, but I'm also frightened.

"I just wanted to stop by," she says, "to apologize for that night. You know the one."

"The night you walked me into a trap?" I ask wryly, standing in the open doorway, crossing my arms over my chest. I don't trust her. I'm certainly not closing the door and muffling the sounds of a potential confrontation.

"You look cute when you're indignant." She laughs. Ghost comes out to investigate, and sniffs at Leigh's flip-flop. Leigh ignores him. "Of course, that's not the real reason I'm here. I thought we should have a little chat."

"About what?" I ask.

The humid air outside wets my back. In the distance, I can hear gulls calling to one another, the voices of fishermen laying crab traps just beyond the tetrapods, the sound of the rolling waves. It sounds so normal, very unlike what is happening in my living room right now.

"Angus," she replies smoothly. "I just wanted to warn you. You can't possibly understand what you're dealing with." She crosses her legs. "He's dangerous, you know."

"No," I snap. "He isn't."

"You, sweet little lamb," Leigh scoffs. "You aren't the same. He has desires you couldn't possibly understand. Even though he pretends he doesn't, he still has instincts, the drive to hunt and kill. To him—to us—you are no better than a pig. Intelligent, sure, but tasty all the same."

"Get out of my house," I snap.

She rests her chin on her palm, surveying me. "You know, he will fuck up eventually. He already has when it comes to you. Y'know, emotions are high and all. Of course he snapped."

Despite the oppressive heat wave, a cold swell pours over my shoulders. "What are you talking about?"

"Your ex tried to break Angus' leg," she says in glee, delighted to be the one breaking the bad news. "So, Angus tried to kill him."

"What?" I just stare at her, mouth agape. It is far too much to process. It's as though I'm standing in the middle of a ring, with two bulls galloping toward me. I can nearly see their keen horns, banderillas fanned across their muscular shoulders. I am not sure which will gore me first. "Is Geoff okay?" I ask, my voice wavering.

"Alive. It's telling that you asked about him first. Either he's the one you really care for, or you're afraid Angus could kill him. It *sort of* goes against your insistence that he's not dangerous." She rises, stretching her long limbs. "Angus is fine, by the way." She walks to the door, patting me on the shoulder. "Good night, Hunter. Think about what I said."

After she leaves, I lock the door and sit in the same spot she occupied moments before. Is she right? Am I pretending that Angus is no different than myself? We are not the same, and this may very well be the writing on the wall. *Angus tried to kill him. Angus tried to kill him... Angus* will *kill him.* Reflexively, I touch my shoulder, upon which the afterimage of his nails remains.

Twenty minutes pass. The doorbell rings. I consider not answering it. I pull my knees up to my chest, wrapping my arms around them. The person at the door hesitates, then knocks. "Hunter?" It's Angus, his voice muffled. "I smell Leigh. Was she here?" I squeeze my eyes shut, resolving to not respond. In truth, I'm terrified.

Without any details, my mind has run amok. I imagine Geoff disemboweled, his innards shiny and slick on the roughly hewn boards of the pier. I imagine his spine broken, his vertebrae at right angles. I imagine his limbs torn away from his body; the remaining stumps akin to raw hamburger meat. I had tried to call Geoff, but the call went to voicemail. *Call me please,* I'd said. *I just want to make sure you are okay. I just… have a bad feeling.*

"I don't know what she told you," Angus's voice wobbles. There was the tiniest part of me that hoped Leigh was lying. But now it is apparent that she was telling the truth. "Please, can we talk?" His voice is gentle, and kind. It's so very unlike the monster I've just painted in my head, using Leigh's brush.

I can't help but to think of the moments where Angus' kind veneer has slipped somewhat: his nails in the flesh of my shoulder; his jaw clenching tight and his nostrils flaring after we kiss; the way he reared back when the words *it's not what you think* spilled from my mouth. I recall the moment when he barged back into the cafe, red-faced and fuming, and how he kissed me so hard I swear he bruised my lips. Even now, they tingle. I can still feel the ghost of his fingers on my cheeks, too. He held me too tight.

I'm frightened. I call Geoff's phone again, but it simply rings and rings until voicemail picks up. *You've reached Geoff Hawkins' phone, leave a message after the beep.*

He's dead, isn't he? The thought makes me sick, and I double over, my head between my knees. Nausea spins the room.

"Okay,' I finally say when I can finally sit upright. I want to see his face. I want to see if he looks like the man who kissed my thighs, his eyes gentle and warm. Conversely, I want to see if he looks like a killer. I think of those old courtroom photos of Ted Bundy. Despite his handsome facade and pressed suit, his eyes were dark and empty like a shark's. I need to look into Angus' eyes. "I'll unlock the door in a minute."

Before I do, I pad to my bedroom and reach up into the dark recesses of the closet, searching for the small lockbox that Geoff had stored there. It's heavy, and I set it on the floor, tapping in the code. 7-1-3-8-7. My birthday. The gun is cold, and I shudder as I curl my fingers around the pommel.

I don't like guns. I never wanted one in the house. I always waved away Geoff's insistence that we go to the shooting range. Carefully, I load the gun. Geoff made sure that I knew how to do that, at least. I hesitate for a moment, deciding whether I should simply empty the chamber and open the door empty-handed. *It's Angus!* Surely, he wouldn't hurt me.

But I never thought he would hurt anyone.

With the weapon dangling in my hand, I return to the living room, slowly opening the front door and stepping aside so that Angus can come in. At first, Angus doesn't notice the weapon. He walks through the threshold looking contrite, limping heavily.

After he closes the door behind himself, I raise the weapon, aiming at his chest. The gun shakes in my grip. "Oh, Hunter." He sighs. "What did she tell you?"

"That you're a fucking monster." I nearly spit the words. They taste badly on my tongue; acidic.

"Baby," he murmurs, his voice soothing as though he's attempting to tame a frightened horse.

"Don't call me that."

"Sorry. *Hunter*. Geoff is fine. He was waiting for me when I left the cafe. He threatened me, and then he attacked me. He would have kept hitting me if I hadn't subdued him."

Leigh said—"

"Leigh says a lot of things." His eyes dart between my face and the gun, uneasily. I use my other hand to steady the gun, shifting my weight to my back foot. Angus' shoulders slump.

"Maybe you should," I spit. I am surprised at how calm I sound. Inside, my heart is breaking. The shards of it stab at my stomach.

"Hunter," he whispers. "I don't want that."

"I don't want to be with you," I reply, pushing the words out in one breath before I can reign them in. "I want you to stay the fuck away from me. I want you to stay away from Geoff. I love him. We're going to get married."

"*Hunter*." Angus steps toward me, but I place the barrel against his sternum. He flinches as though I've slipped a knife into him. And haven't I? I've unequivocally chosen Geoff. "I really care about you," he continues. "I'm not like James."

"From where I'm standing, you're *just* like him." I think of James stepping close to me, his face in sharp relief against the bonfire.

Angus scrubs at his face with his palm. His dark hair sticks to his forehead, a sheen of sweat on his brow. "You don't mean that," he says.

"Don't tell me what I fucking think," I snarl. "This is your one warning, Stay away from Geoff. I don't want to see you in my cafe ever again." I jab him hard with the gun, and he steps backward, arms raised.

"Okay," he finally relents. "I hear you." He carefully steps over Ghost, who despite the tense situation, has entwined himself around his legs. "I'm going. Please don't shoot me in the back." He slowly pivots and walks to the door. His movements deliberate, he opens the door slowly and steps out. But, before he goes, he turns to look at me. It's apparent that he thinks it may very well be for the last time. "I really think I could have loved you someday," he whispers, then he's gone, jogging down the lane toward his grandmother's house.

Chapter Fifteen
(ANGUS)

———⊲◆⊳———

"What happened?" Ama asks as I mount the porch steps. My hands are tingling, each joint taut as if mid-squeeze. She's always been perceptive. The old woman leans back in her rocking chair until the runners tip off the ground, then lets the momentum drive her forward, and back, forward, and back, it's a chaotic gesture, but the only way she can pretend to run. Even with four paws, she is stricken with ever-worsening arthritis. "You look pale," she observes.

"Granny," I whisper, holding out my hands as if in supplication. "I couldn't stop myself."

"What did you do?" The rocking stops, her feet planted firmly on the floorboards. "Quickly, child. Speak."

"I got into a fight and nearly killed the other guy." I slowly ease myself down onto the porch steps, rolling my pant leg up to examine my knee. The swelling has made the skin shiny and stretched, and I fear if I poke it that it will pop like a balloon. "He started it," I mumble, knowing it's no excuse.

"I told you that I didn't want any trouble," she replies, her tone stern, measured. "That was the deal."

Her fierce, albeit rheumy eyes bore into mine. I wish I could have seen her in her heyday, leading her pack with grit and unmatched passion. She was serious, bordering on acerbity. She was strong, capable of felling even the hardiest of foes.

Ama was — is — the quintessential Alpha.

"I know."

"Were you wolfish?"

"No, no. Nothing like that." I am suddenly very aware of the acute pain in my knuckles, the skin there bruised and broken. "I hurt him pretty badly, but I don't think anything will come of it. He... he got what he wanted." I think of Hunter, the revolver shaking in his hands. The prey became the huntsman.

"Between you and James, I should make you leave. But you're my grandson. My—" her voice catches, and she coughs. The sound is moist as though her lungs are full of water. "—only family."

I met Ama for the first time at my mother's funeral. Before then, she was just a thing of legend, as distant from me as a queen is from the serfs. But, at the funeral, she was just a small woman with red-rimmed eyes and shaking hands, who leaned over my mother's casket, whispering to her. "They made her look nice," she had said to me, afterward. "You can barely see the scars."

"Don't let this happen again," Ama continues. "Or...I'll use the last of my strength to eat you."

"I love you," I tell her, reaching out to grasp her hand.

Ama squeezes my fingers for a moment, then leans back in her chair. Her eyes close. "Now leave me alone so I can nap," she mutters.

"Let's go out," I announce as I barrel through the front door. My heart is hammering, but I decide to channel it into self-destruction. I would never tell the pack—I wouldn't give them the satisfaction—but I'm heartbroken. Hunter is getting back together with his ex. He made that abundantly clear. *It's not what it looks like.* I should have strangled Geoff for one minute more, then pushed him into the ocean to be picked apart by fish.

"Out where?" Luka asks, not looking up from the ratty copy of *1984* he found amongst Ama's things. He sits sideways on the chair, his legs thrown over the armrest. His locs are loose, spilling over his shoulders. "Why do you sound like that?"

"Somewhere with cheap alcohol," I reply. "How do I sound?"

"Cheerful," he says. "Too cheerful." He looks up from his book. "Like artificially cheerful. Are you okay?"

"Fake it until you make it," I say wryly. I hobble into the guest room, and find James there, dozing with his forearm over his eyes.

"Get up," I say, slapping him on the thigh. "We're going out!"

James groans. "I'm sleeping, Gus." I feel like I've lived three lives while James napped, entirely unaffected by the goings-ons. Which is ironic because all of this is effectively his fault.

"It's not even 9 o'clock. Come on. We're going to this little dive bar I know." I pick through the piles of clothes on the floor for a clean-ish pair of jeans and a fresh tee. I have difficulty putting on the jeans over my stiff knee, which is the size of a baseball. I hiss in pain. James lifts his arm just enough to look at me. "What happened to you?" he asks.

"A fight," I snap.

"A fight?" James sits up, clearly interested. "With whom?"

"You don't know him," I reply coolly. "Are you coming to the bar or not?"

"I'm definitely coming."

The Barracks is a gay bar, tucked between a clothing store and an empty storefront. We walk in single file, and I point out an unoccupied booth near the window. It's dim inside, the windows opaque and textured as though shaped from crushed glass. It's not all that dissimilar from my recollection of it. I walked in once when I was sixteen. On my first visit, I only got so far as the vestibule before a bouncer asked for my ID. But what I saw became ingrained in my memory: people being unabashedly themselves, smiling and dancing.

"What does everyone want to drink?" I ask, shouting over the din. The bar is crowded, and music pumps through the speakers; the floor shakes with it.

"Just a beer. Whatever is on tap," Luka says.

"Long Island," Leigh says, wiggling her eyebrows. I have a difficult time looking at her. She told Hunter what happened. Though I concede, it's doubtful that she affected the outcome. Hunter would have still felt betrayed, frightened. He simply may not have had the foresight to point a gun at my heart.

"Absolutely not," I snort. "We are already on thin ice with Ama."

"Come on," Leigh whines. "I'll be good. Promise."

James laughs. "I won't bail you out tonight if you're arrested," he tells his sister. "I'll order you something nice."

"*Fiiiiiiine*," she says, drawing out the vowel. She crosses her arms. "But I'm not happy about it."

"Noted," I reply coolly. I head toward the bar, and James follows suit. He casually takes my elbow, helping to steer me through the crowd. I am secretly grateful for it; my knee is throbbing, and the pain blurs my senses somewhat. *Fuck you, Geoff.* When we order our drinks, James adds two shots of Jäger.

"You need it," he says. "You look like shit."

"Thanks," I deadpan. We clink glasses and down them in unison. I wince. I've always hated the taste of licorice. We gather the drinks—holding two each—and return to the table. Without James' help, I am slow, and the trip back takes twice as long. At the table, we chat about largely banal things: Leigh's plan to sun herself on the beach tomorrow, Luka's desire to enroll at the community college, and our plans to potentially buy a large apartment in the town proper. No one mentions my altercation with Geoff.

"I want to dance," Leigh says, popping out of the booth. "C'mon Luka."

"I don't—" Luka starts, but she grabs his wrist, hauling him to his feet. "Leigh!" he whines, before he's forcibly yanked into the milieu. I sigh, pressing the heels of my hands into my eyes until starbursts appear. I want to squash the image of Hunter from my retinas, shaking as he holds the revolver in both hands.

"Are you okay?" James murmurs. He's sitting beside me, and he rests his hand on my shoulder.

"No," I admit. I take a sip of my whiskey sour.

"I'm sorry." I'm not sure what exactly he's apologizing for. *I'm sorry for making us leave Portland. I'm sorry for attacking Hunter. I'm sorry you're hurting.* "What happened today?"

"After you left the cafe, you mean?" I'm still angry at him, and I don't want him to forget his part in it. For once, he remains quiet, and I continue, longing to fill the silence; longing to push the memories out of my head. *Here, James, carry this for me.* "Hunter's boyfriend saw me—us. So, he attacked me." I stretch my stiff knee out under the table.

"You let him?" James asks, raising a perfect eyebrow. His lips twitch into a self-satisfied smirk.

"No," I reply. "I didn't *let* him do anything. He surprised me. But then, I lost control." I look down at my bruised, cracked knuckles. "I thought I was going to kill him. I almost did. I wanted to." I sigh, watching condensation trickling down the sides of my glass. "Hunter is marrying him," I say, before I can stop myself. I expect James to crow, make fun, say "I told you so," but instead, he slips an arm around my shoulders.

"At least," he says slowly. "Geoff probably won't remember his wedding, what with the concussion you gave him."

A guffaw bursts from me, and I immediately feel chagrined. It feels taboo to laugh today. I tip the rest of my drink down my throat and lean into James' body. The Jäger warms my belly and the whiskey sour follows suit. It deadens my pain. "I'm still angry," I mutter. "At you."

"I know," he whispers. James sips his White Russian, the thick cream clinging to his upper lip and making him appear mustachioed. He licks it away. "I'm sorry."

Suddenly, Luka appears. He has his half-finished beer in hand, and he moves his hips to the music. "Come dance with us!" He gestures at Leigh, who is swaying animatedly to *Body Work,* her arms in the air.

You do your body work; I feel my pulse working overtime...

"Dance?" James asks me, the corner of his lips twitching. He's trying very hard not to laugh. He doesn't dance.

"We'll pass, Lu," I tell the younger man.

"We aren't giving up that easily!" Luka says, making a come-hither motion as he steps back into the crowd. It's as though it's a threat. *Have fun, or else!* But I *am* having fun. Sitting with my husband feels nice, and talking so frankly feels even better.

"I really am," James says after a moment of silence. "Sorry, I mean."

"I know," I say, looking at him.

He looks handsome tonight. His salt-and-pepper hair is, per usual, coiffed; nary a hair out of place. I hate that my breath catches when I look at him, even still. I'm heartbroken over Hunter, I remind myself. Maybe that's why I desperately want James to hold me tonight. When we took down that doe, we worked in tandem, mirror images. I knew how he would move, where his paws would land. I knew the trajectory of his jaws. And when I strangled Geoff, I knew the part of him that had been a stranger. We are inextricably bound.

James leans close. I can smell the coffee and vodka on his breath. It reminds me of the cafe, the way Hunter's hair smelled. "I want to kiss you," he murmurs, cupping the back of my neck. Our knees touch, and his hand rests firmly on my upper thigh. "I don't expect us to get back together. I don't know if you'd want to—or even if I would deserve it. But tonight? Tonight, I want to kiss you."

Looking down the barrel of the gun made me feel so alone. I was cast aside like a stray dog. But James—imperfect, complicated, infuriating James— still wants me. I lean forward and kiss him, grateful for the familiarity. Kissing him is like putting on a well-worn sweater. When he deepens the kiss, I melt into him with a small moan. I lose myself in him. The bar and its patrons are obscured, and muffled, by a rolling fog. "James," I groan into his mouth.

James nips my lip and I gasp. "If we weren't in public—" he says, but he needn't finish the sentence. I want him, too. His eyes flick around the room. "Come on," he prompts, his voice desperate. He leads the way through the crowd, gripping my hand tight. We pass Luka on the dance floor, his hands around the waist of a handsome brunette. Leigh sits at the bar, legs crossed, chatting with the bartender. Neither notice us, too engrossed in their own dalliances.

The bathroom is empty, and, with the door closed, the noises of The Barracks fade. We nearly topple into a bathroom stall, tearing at each other's clothes with wild abandon. James unbuttons my jeans, pulling them down just enough to spring free my already stiffening cock. He firmly encircles it with his hand, and I sigh.

"You like that?" he growls.

"Oh god," I whisper. "Yeah, baby."

James presses me back against the partition, expertly working my cock. "I'm going to fuck you," he hisses into my ear. "right here."

Grasping my shoulder, he roughly turns me to face the wall, slamming my cheek against the partition. I growl. The sound of metal on metal and the rustling of fabric tells me he is unbuckling his belt and pulling down his pants, I look over my shoulder and watch as he spits into his hand, stroking his turgid cock until it becomes slick and shiny.

Despite myself, I think of Hunter on his bed, his doe eyes as he watched me slide into his heat. Do I look the same to James? But then, James is inside me and he roughly fists my hair. I plant my palms against the plastic laminate, groaning as he thrusts. He pulls my head back so that he can watch my lips tremble, and my eyes squeeze shut.

Chapter Fifteen (angus)

The door of the bathroom opens, and inside the stall, we freeze. Someone enters the stall beside ours, coughs, then takes a piss.

Unbothered by the intrusion, James continues to slowly fuck me, clapping his rough hand over my mouth. "Be quiet," he whispers, licking the soft flesh of my earlobe. "Be a good boy." He presses me hard against the partition, rocking into and out of me. Finally, the toilet flushes, the sink runs, and the door opens and closes. "C'mere," James commands, sliding out of me "Let me see that pretty face." He's toying with me. He thinks I'm *his*.

"You're fucking insufferable," I snort. "That's your problem. You never know when to shut up."

"Yeah," James agrees, shrugging his broad shoulders. He grasps both of our cocks in one hand, stroking them in tandem. I arch my hips. *More, more!* I try very hard not to think of Hunter. I try very hard not to think of how good it was to feel Geoff's heartbeat quicken beneath my palms. "Well, you married me. So, what does that make you?"

Chapter Sixteen
(HUNTER)

———◁♦▷———

I dream of Angus and wake up next to Geoff.

In the pearl-gray light of morning, I lay awake, staring at the specter of my old life. If Geoff were to rouse himself, I would roll away and pretend to be asleep. But, for the moment, I unabashedly stare. His mouth is agape, loud snores reverberating through his body and the mattress beneath. The surgery swelled his sinuses, and he has been sleeping fitfully. He will often wake up with a gasp, thrashing for a moment before returning to his slumber. The flesh beneath his left eye is black with a corona of purple.

It will get worse before it gets better. Maybe the same is true of our relationship.

I slowly ease out of bed, padding barefoot into the kitchen. I can't go back to sleep. Ghost sashays in, sniffing at his empty food bowl.

He meows as if to say *feed me*.

I fill the bowl with kibble and the kettle with water. "Good morning," I tell the cat. "Did you sleep well?" My voice sounds remarkably hollow, devoid of emotion.

I feel as though I'm sleepwalking and have been since I held that gun four weeks ago. I've been going through the motions. I offered to let Geoff stay with me to recover; let him climb atop me when he started to feel better ("C'mon baby, just like that"); and when he asked a second time, I accepted his proposal. I used to be so sure that this was where we were heading, and now being here feels disingenuous.

As I fill the French press with boiling water, I think of Angus doing the same in this very kitchen. *Why can't I stop thinking about him?* He brutalized Geoff. "He just wouldn't stop," Geoff told me, tearfully. "He came out of nowhere." I push down the plunger and pour the coffee into a mug. It's one of the rejects. One of the many that Geoff tossed aside angrily, refusing to either paint or glaze it. I liked to rescue the cast offs and finish them myself. On this one, I had painted a seagull, which turned out horribly misshapen. A Franken-Gull.

The coffee makes my synapses fire, dumping dopamine throughout my system. I nearly convince myself that my feelings were little more than early morning existentialism. But then Geoff walks into the kitchen. He yawns, stretching until his shoulders crack. I cringe. I hate that sound and he knows that. *How many times have I said it?*

"Morning," he mumbles, reaching for the French press, pouring himself a cup. *I'll need to brew more, thanks for asking.*

"Hey," I manage. *I wish I could feel happy.*

"You're up early," he remarks. He sets his mug on the tabletop and bends at the waist to kiss my temple with dry lips.

"I have to get to the cafe early. María starts today." María is one of Renee's friends from the community college and a near constant presence in the cafe after days spent in the theater department's black box. She would often arrive with exaggerated makeup, meant to be seen even from the cheap seats. *I'm Evita*, she would say by way of explanation, rolling her eyes and wiping at the blush with a napkin. Renee had been hounding me to hire her for months, and I finally relented.

"It doesn't open for another hour and a half," Geoff observes, glancing at the clock. "Want to have break-fast together?" What he really means is *Hunter, make me breakfast*. I'm not in the mood. I can't muster the energy.

I rise, taking my mug to the sink. The coffee inside sloshes as I place it therein. I only drank half. "I have to do a few things," I say over my shoulder. "There's eggs and cereal. Help yourself."

Geoff snags my wrist as I pass him, pulling me to a halt. "Hunter," he says. "Are you okay?"

"Yeah, yeah. I'll see you after work." I shrug him off and gather my things in the living room: keys, wallet... *where's my phone?* I search under the coffee table, between the couch cushions, even in the alcove where Ghost hides her toys. Geoff stands in the doorway, watching me.

"Are you angry at me?" he asks uneasily.

"No," I say, searching under the couch. I pull out one of my socks and an enormous dust bunny. No phone.

"You've just seem... cold." I didn't think he had noticed. He's always been so self-centered. Once, he found me weeping in the bathroom, having just received news that my grandfather had died. *We can still go to the Kahlo exhibit tonight, right?* he asked while running his palm up and down my spine in a conciliatory manner.

"I'm fine," I snap. I rise and turn in a slow circle. Where is it, where is it, *where is it?* Have I lost it?

"You're happy right? With me?" His eyes are watery, and his lip trembles.

"What are you talking about?" Agitated, I pull all of the cushions off the couch, tossing them onto the carpet. I just want to go to work. If I answer those questions truthfully—if I even allow myself to *think* of the answers, I will destroy everything. I will be the Enola Gay releasing the atom bomb from her belly.

"You've barely smiled in weeks," Geoff replies, his Adam's Apple bobbing as he swallows. "Please tell me you aren't still thinking about him." His voice wobbles, and he sniffs.

Angus. "I'm not," I reply too quickly. I may as well have slapped Geoff in the face.

His face turns blotchy and red, and he presses his lips together. "Right."

"Right, *what?*"

"You are thinking about him," he spits. "What do you want from me, Hunter? I proposed, just like you wanted, even though I didn't want to."

"That's great," I scoff. "Are you just planning to placate me—hoping that I shut up about marriage now that I have a ring on my finger? Unbelievable."

"Fuck you, Hunt. You don't get to attack me. You're the one daydreaming about that violent asshole. He tried to *kill* me, remember?"

"I'm not—"

"Go to work," he growls, waving me away. "By the way, your phone is charging on the bedside table."

✦ ✦ ✦

Geoff's admission that he never planned—nor wanted—to marry me rolls around in my belly. I feel sick. I make it midway down the boardwalk toward Main Street before I turn back. I'm not sure where I'm going until I get there: Ama Chilton's bungalow. During my first time here, I barely gave it a second glance, too absorbed in seeing Angus. Someone's swim trunks dry on the porch railing. A terracotta pot, overcrowded with wilting daisies, sits near the stairs. A welcome mat exclaiming "Wipe Your Paws!" greets me at the front door, two swipes of sand marring its textured surface.

It all seems so normal, no different than any other home on Bird's Nest. No one would ever suspect it housed anything supernatural.

I knock. I try to convince myself I only need to look into Angus' eyes one more time. I need to convince myself that pushing forward with Geoff isn't a mistake. *You know it is*, I admonish myself. *Geoff has never been The One.*

When the door opens, it isn't Angus. It's James. My stomach flip-flops, and I step backward. "Oh!" I exclaim. He is naked, a towel wrapped loosely around his waist. His hair, still damp, hangs limply upon his forehead.

"What do you want?" he asks. "It's six in the fucking morning." It's as though I'm little more than an annoyance. I may as well be a traveling salesman, touting my wares.

"I—" My voice shakes, and I clench my fists tight. I don't like that I sound so frightened. But James frightens me. He still haunts the dreams I never quite remember when I wake. "I need to see Angus."

"He's asleep," James replies coolly. "He isn't interested in seeing you, pitiful human."

"I need to talk to him," I insist.

James chuckles, the act entirely changing his features. He no longer looks stony-faced and pugnacious. Instead, I can see the allure that must have drawn Angus to him. "And I *said* he doesn't want to see you. He's perfectly occupied with me."

With him. "Wha—"

Abruptly, James steps toward me, his hand encircling the nape of my neck to pull me close. I wonder if he can feel the shiny skin there, newly healed. Can he still smell the infinitesimal remains of my dried blood under his fingernails? "Let me elucidate: Angus doesn't want someone like you." James leans close, his breath hot and spittle wetting my face. "He doesn't even think about you."

The sick feeling—present since I woke this morning—intensifies. I really think I may vomit. It was a mistake to come here. Despite the words he said in anger, it's unfair to Geoff. Discovering that Angus is back with the man who tried to kill me is akin to a right hook to the jaw.

"I'm leaving," I manage, but James doesn't release me. My heart hammers. *Can he hear it beating? Are his ears that keen?*

"Stay away from my husband." His teeth elongate, grotesquely filling his mouth, and I whimper. "Or I'll finish the job," he continues. "There won't even be enough of you to put in a casket."

Our noses nearly touching, a low, guttural growl escapes him. It is an inhuman sound.

"Okay, okay. Please, just let me go." When he does as I ask, I stumble backward, tumbling down the porch steps head over foot. The ground rushes up to pummel me. *Oomph.* I scramble to my feet, not bothering to wipe the sand from my behind. "I'm going." I am ashamed of it, but I run away, arms pumping. I run until I reach Main Street, sweat staining the back of my tee and dripping into my eyes.

Renee and María loiter outside of the coffee shop, smoking cigarettes. They look so perfectly normal, blissfully unaware of the horrors that lurk in Wharton, Renee's lips purse and her eyebrows furrow when she spots me. "I didn't take you for a jogger."

"Yeah," I say, panting, my hands on my knees. "I'm not."

"I guess you've got to get in shape for your wedding," María says. "Congratulations, by the way."

"Yeah," I mumble. "Let's open up."

♦ ♦ ♦

When we close up shop in the late afternoon, I press a key into Renee's hand. "Here you go, Assistant Manager."

Renee's eyes widen, and she throws her arms around me in a tight hug. Her body vibrates with emotion. "Are you serious?" she breathes into the curve of my neck. Renee releases me, her cheeks a deep crimson.

"Of course," I reply. "Someone has to man the place if I ever take a day off."

"Unlikely," Renee snorts. "I'm sure you'll come in even on your wedding day." The ring on my finger burns like a hot iron. I wish I hadn't told anyone about the proposal. But, for the briefest moment, I really believed I could be happy. I blamed my feelings of trepidation on nerves. *After all,* I told myself, *getting married is a big deal, an entirely new chapter.*

"True, but maybe. Someday." I pat the brick wall of my building, overcome by a swell of affection. Ebb and Flow is my lifeblood. Wharton, too. "I'll see you two tomorrow."

The girls practically skip down the sidewalk, arm-and-arm, talking animatedly. I am always surprised by the energy of the very young. Conversely, I trudge down the sidewalk, my joints aching terribly. The milk steamer burned the back of my hand this morning, and my flesh feels hot and tight. Today has been a bad day.

Then, I hear his voice.

The baby hairs on the back of my neck stand up. A shiver ripples down my spine.

Angus walks on the opposite sidewalk, balancing on the edge of the curb. He is with Luka, who is stopping outside of every restaurant, reading the menus pinned to their respective sidewalk signs. "This one might be good. Oh, look, this one has all-day breakfast," the younger man says. Angus makes noncommittal noises.

I pause, unabashedly staring. Pedestrians walk around me, grumbling, but I don't notice. I want to call out to him, to ensnare the attention of those blue eyes. But the words I had meant to speak this morning have escaped me. All I can think about is James' teeth and Geoff's squared jaw. *Keep walking, Hunter!* But I can't seem to move. I may as well have grown roots.

"Angus," I call out, croaking around the lump in my throat.

Angus' eyes meet mine. He shoves his hands into his pockets, hunching his shoulders. He chews at his bottom lip.

Luka hasn't noticed me. He reads the menu of Dottie's Diner. "This place has milkshakes. Let's eat here."

"Go get a table," Angus says, out of the corner of his mouth. "I've got to do something first."

Luka looks up and spots me. "Angus—" He sighs.

"—go on," Angus insists. "Five minutes."

"If you're a minute over, I'm ordering without you," Luka replies. He heads inside Dottie's, shaking his head.

Through the window, I watch the eponymous Dottie rush to greet him, her smile like a beacon calling him home. *Come in, child, what can I make for you today?*

Angus steps off the curb, slowly walking across the street toward me. "Hey," he murmurs.

"Aren't you afraid I'm going to shoot you?" I ask.

"Are you planning on shooting me?" he asks evenly.

"No." I can't help but to grin. "I don't plan to."

He steps up onto the curb. I step back. It's an impulse; I'm not afraid as much as I'm worried that I'll do something I'll regret. I want to touch him. *God, I desperately want to touch him.* His hair is bundled at the base of his neck, errant strands bursting from the knot. I can't help but to imagine pulling off the elastic, letting his hair settle around his broad shoulders. I want to run my fingers through it.

"I came to see you today," I say. My lips suddenly feel dry, and I lick them. "But James told me to 'fuck off.'"

"That sounds like him."

"He said you were back together." I can't hide the hurt in my voice.

Angus snorts, his nostrils flaring. "Not in the slightest. I heard you were getting married." There's no accusation there. It's simply a statement, with a question implicit therein. *Are you getting married?*

"I—" I press my lips together. "I was taking care of Geoff after—after what happened. He asked me to marry him, and I said yes. But—"

"But?"

"I'm not happy," I reply, slowly, tasting the words. It's the first time I've verbalized the dark thought I've been harboring. The sidewalk is becoming crowded as would-be bar hoppers head toward Jefferson, and Angus steps closer to me so that they can pass us by. It's as though we are an archipelago in a tumultuous sea. His knuckles brush against my wrist. Something inside my core tightens.

"I'm not happy either," Angus replies. "Hunter, I fucked up. One hundred percent. There's no excuse. It doesn't matter that Geoff attacked me; I should have walked away."

He came out of nowhere, Geoff had said. "You attacked him, Angus."

Angus shakes his head. "No. I was walking home, and he was waiting for me. He nearly broke my kneecap and then I lost control." I think of Angus' pronounced limp when he walked into my home two months ago. A thought bubbles up in my mind: *Geoff wasn't capable of hurting Angus without the element of surprise.* A flash of white-hot anger nearly overpowers me. Geoff lied to me. And I nearly shot Angus in retribution.

"Oh god. Angus—" I reach out for his hand, and he squeezes it. He may as well have said *it's okay, I forgive you* with that one simple gesture. "Geoff lied to me."

Geoff has always been a complicated, clearly egocentric person, but I never thought him capable of a bald-faced lie. I certainly didn't expect him to ever lie to me outright.

"Hey." Angus touches my cheek. "You didn't know. it wasn't wrong to hate me."

"I don't want to hate you," I insist. "I want..." *But what do I want?*

I want to leave my engagement ring on my bedside table. I want to kiss the man standing here now, his eyes searching mine. I want to loosen his hair from its tether and hold it in my fist. Slowly, excruciatingly so, I stand on my tiptoes to kiss his mouth. It's a restrained kiss, our lips barely grazing.

Angus cups my head between his hands. "What do you want, Hunter? I want to give you exactly what you want."

God.

"Come with me to the cafe," I reply.

"Putting me to work, hmm?" His smile is coy, and my cheeks burn. "Let me blow off Luka, and then we can go wherever you'd like."

◆ ◆ ◆

I don't bother to turn on the lights. I know the cafe better than the back of my hand. Once the door is locked behind us, Angus sits at one of the tables. He rests his chin on his palm. "What would you like now?" There's a suggestion therein. He wants me to make the decision I never quite got to make for myself.

"This is where you kissed me for the first time," I stand over him, gently stroking his hair. His palms alight on my hips, pulling me between his thighs.

The streetlight outside illuminates three quarters of his facade. "You kissed me."

"Did I?" I suppose it doesn't matter. "I want to do it again." In the darkness, I feel brave. I'm not typically forward, nor the dominant personality in any relationship, romantic or otherwise. Certainly not when it comes to intimacy. I bend down to press my lips against his. I can't help but to think of the magic that mouth is capable of.

Angus pulls me down onto his lap, and I wrap my arms around his neck. "What do you want?" he repeats.

The corner of his lip twitches into a coy smile. *He is enjoying this.*

"Shut up," I whisper, covering his mouth with mine.

Finally, I free his hair from the elastic, and it curls around his face, a veritable mane. I gather it into my fist, pulling his head back so that I can kiss the stubbly flesh of his jaw. His Adam's Apple bobs as he gasps. Angus grasps my ass and grinds his hips into mine. He's already so desperately hard. I can feel him even through the thick fabric of his jeans. Geoff never wanted me like this. Geoff never really wanted me at all.

"On the table," Angus gasps. "God, Hunter, I can't wait."

"Patience," I tell him, surprised at the evenness of my voice. I slowly shuck his shirt up over his head, revealing his broad chest with its downy fur. I kiss his clavicle, tasting the salt on his skin with my tongue. Angus' fingertips trail up and down my spine, little moans escaping his parted lips. I kiss his shoulder, brushing the pads of my thumbs over his pink nipples until they become stiff.

Gooseflesh follows my kisses down his abdomen as I slide off of his lap. "Hunter!" For the briefest moment, Angus' voice changes. It's reminiscent of the voice he spoke with at the bonfire, the voice of the wolf that resides within him. And his eyes! Despite the darkness, his eyes glow. But when he blinks, his face is, again, cast in shadow. I unbuckle his pants, and he helps me pull them off of his muscular thighs. His cock tents his underwear, and I kiss him through the fabric.

He bucks his hips. "I'll rip those clothes off of you," he growls, trembling with desire.

"Patience," I remind him. I kiss the spot just below his belly button, my tongue dragging down his belly until I reach the waistband of his boxer briefs. Angus arches his back, stroking my hair with his hands. He's begging for it. I feel powerful, the little lamb conquering the lion. I peel his boxers down, his cock springing free. It's swollen with desire, precum beading on the tip. I wrap my hand around it, stroking him.

"That's so good," Angus groans as I run my thumb over his slit. His mouth slack, he watches me. "So fucking good." After a moment, he places his hand over mine. His eyes flash again, and he blinks it away. "Take off your clothes." I rise, turning away from him to unbutton my flannel shirt. "No. Hunter, please. Let me see."

I turn back. He's nearly panting with longing, and now, his eyes glow unabated. For a moment, genuine fear courses through me. But the hands reaching toward me are gentle. "Your eyes," I manage.

"You're torturing me," he replies drolly. "Do you trust me?"

I swallow. It may be my imagination, but, in the shadows, his face takes on a sort of amorphous quality. Am I seeing things, or are his ears pointed? I reach out and touch them. They are, and the downy flesh therein is thick and velvety. A low whine escapes his throat at my touch. "Yes," I whisper. "I trust you."

"Take it all off," he implores. "Please." I do as he asks, stripping out of my jeans and boxer briefs. His breath hitches as he looks at me. "God, I nearly forgot how beautiful you are."

I am glad that it's too dark for him to see me blush. Or can he? *Those eyes.* Suddenly, Angus is on his feet, his body pressed tightly against mine. It's as though I blinked, and he was here, breathing the same air. He kisses me, hard, his tongue spilling inro my mouth. His tooth clips my lip and a tiny sunspot of pain bursts on my periphery. His gentle touch is a salve. Abruptly, he lifts me off my feet without so much as a word, placing me on the countertop. My hip bumps against the register and the cash drawer pops out. *Ca-ching!*

CHAPTER SEVENTEEN
(GEOFF)

———◁◆▷———

Hunter should have been off work an hour ago. I pace back-and-forth on our porch, swatting the mosquitos that alight on my arms. It's surprisingly cool tonight. Soon, the mosquitos will die off. *Thank god.* I roll my tight shoulders, craning my neck so that I can look up and down Bird's Nest. There's no sign of Hunter. Despite the encroaching darkness, I know that I could identify him by silhouette alone. He walks with reckless abandon, swinging his arms like a kid spotting a playground. Though, recently, he moves with the enthusiasm of a zombie. That is, with no ardor at all.

I shouldn't have told him the proposal was meant to placate him. But he's been so surly. I wanted to hurt him as much as he's been hurting me. It was childish of me, but he's been acting like a child, too. He thinks that I can't see his relentless scowl, the way his eyes slide away from my face during sex. I sink into the Adirondack chair, resting my elbows on the armrests.

I text Candy.

[Geoff: Where is your brother?]
Several minutes Later, Candy replies.
[Candy: How should I know?]
[Geoff: Is he still at the cafe? Are the lights on?]
She will be annoyed with my persistence, but I know she'll open the window and check. If the lights are on, she will see the warm glow cutting the sidewalk in twain.

[Candy: Nope. The lights are out. Maybe he stopped for groceries.]
[Geoff: Maybe.]
I sigh, resting my chin on my palm. I don't share my secret worry with her. *What if he doesn't come home at all?* Or, worse, *what if he does and he asks me to move out again?* Candy is one of my closest friends, but I know I overstayed my welcome at the loft. She had started to theatrically sigh when she would find me on the couch, stepping over my legs so that she could sit down, too.

"You're Geoff, right?" A man sidles up to the porch, startling me. He's tall and broad, his flesh decorated in intricate tattoos. I recognize him, but I can't quite pinpoint from where nor when. My memory has been so bad since the attack.

That's what I've been calling it: an attack. *He attacked me,* I told the EMT, the nurses in the ER, and Candy when she came to take me home. At first, I was too ashamed to admit my part in it. Then, I luxuriated in their sympathy. When Hunter came, throwing himself across my chest, sobbing apologies, I knew I would never speak the truth aloud. I wouldn't even *think* it.

"That's me," I reply, straightening in my chair. "Who's asking?"

"It doesn't matter," the man says. "But let's say we have a mutual friend." The man rests his elbows on the porch rail, surveying me. "Did you ever wonder how your fiancé got those scars on his neck?"

Werewolves! Or so Hunter had said. Now, if I dare ask, he just shakes his head hard, like he's trying to joggle the memories out of his skull. The man doesn't wait for an answer. "He's right, you know. There are wolves in Wharton."

I can't help but to laugh. The man shrugs his muscular shoulders. "I can prove it." He grins, his bright, white teeth catching the porch light. Why do they look so sharp? "But, maybe, you should have Angus show you."

"What are you talking about?" The stranger is making me feel uneasy. Angus' name makes me feel overwrought. I have nightmares about him, sometimes, with his savage eyes and violent hands. I had blamed it on the asphyxia, but I could have sworn his pupils had grown overly large like a predator's.

"Go to the cafe," the man says. "You'll see the wolf of Wharton." The man gives me a little wave, before slipping his hands in his pockets and continuing down the road.

"Wait!" I call out, leaping to my feet. The sudden movement makes my vision swim and my head ache terribly, an aftereffect of the skull fracture. "Shouldn't you call Animal Control or something?"

The man laughs. "You have a gun, don't you?"

After he leaves, I sit on the porch for a long while. It bothers me that I know him. *Where do I know him from?* I think of the demon on his throat, picturing it in my mind's eye until it contorts into a great red wolf.

The Wolf of Wharton, he had said.

♦ ♦ ♦

"Love, huh?" the man says, watching idly as I storm out of Ebb and Flow. He gestures at the cafe with an unlit cigarette. I take off my glasses, swiping at encroaching tears with the back of my hand. I wish I could wipe away the image of Hunter kissing someone else, too.

"Go fuck yourself," I spit. The man's jocular tone infuriates me. I'm also not in the mood to talk to strangers. I am rudderless, unsure where to go or what to do. I want to go home and throw Hunter's clothes out on the lawn. I want to storm back into the cafe, and punch Angus in the gut. I want to sink under the ground. I want to fly up into the stratosphere until it gets hard to breathe.

"I'm going to have to," the man chortles. "The other one in there is my husband. You look just how I feel." He lights his cigarette and takes a drag, tilting his head back to release the smoke from his mouth. His neck is adorned with a red tattoo, though I can't quite make it out. A rose, perhaps?

"Can I get one of those?" I ask, gesturing at the cigarette. It's as though his admission has knotted us together. We are a lonely club of two. Though, somehow, knowing I'm not the only one makes me feel worse.

"Sure," the man says, reaching into his breast pocket for a pack of cigarettes. I pop the filter between my lips, and he lights it for me. "You don't deserve this, you know."

"You don't either," I reply glumly. The man and I watch as Angus leaves the cafe and speed-walks toward the pier. I clench my teeth, blowing menthol smoke out of my nostrils. I want to kill him. I've never wanted to kill someone before. The thought doesn't even frighten me.

"I'm not going to stop you," the man says. I raise my eyebrows, not comprehending. "If you need to teach him a lesson," he clarifies, the cigarette bobbing in his mouth. "You'd better catch him by surprise — kick the legs right out from under him."

CHAPTER EIGHTEEN
(ANGUS)

———◁♦▷———

My body feels like a taut string. Every time Hunter looks at me with those big glassy eyes, a twang reverberates through me. My skin tingles; my wolfishness threatens to burst forth. Hunter's hand stroking my upturned ear was nearly too much. He wasn't afraid. When I lift him and place him on the countertop, I have to stop myself from leaping atop him. I don't want to be gentle. I want to fuck. But that isn't what Hunter needs from me right now.

I kiss him, stepping between his legs. I stroke his silken length, my grip firm. I know that, for him, each caress feels like torment. It's a good kind of anticipation, like opening a gift. I try very hard not to look at the ring on his finger, a burnished gold band clearly crafted by an artisan's hands. Or rather, by an artisan-in-training. It's uneven, its shank a discordant blend of convex and concave. I had heard that he was seeing Geoff again. Marrying him. It's hard not to hear bits and pieces; in a sense, they are Wharton's *It* Couple.

The one the denizens most root for. *The carefree artist and the barista. What a pair!* Barf.

"Angus," Hunter pants. "What if someone sees?" From here, I can see into the street via the picture window, and, potentially, a passerby could see me, too. *I saw the barista with a dark stranger who* isn't *his fiancé.* Still, I want to say, *let them watch. Let them gossip.* He sits up, coiling his fingers in my hair. "The back room—"

Hunter slides off the counter and pads through the door, his cock pointing the way. I follow, starting at his dimpled ass. We walk into a large space with concrete floors and shelves upon which are stacked bags of coffee beans and other accouterments. A humming industrial refrigerator stands in the corner. Once we are through the threshold, I crush his mouth with mine, impatient.

With gentle, probing fingers, I ease the tension from his neck. He presses into my hands, little sighs emanating from his parted lips. His cock presses against my thigh, the muscles quavering. I like how he reacts to my touch. Every part of him succumbs as if he's never been touched before. I can't help but to think of the sounds of lovemaking I heard the night of the attack. He certainly didn't make these sounds— panting, gasping, moaning—with Geoff.

Hunter sinks to his knees at my feet, his hands running up my thighs. "Does that feel good?" he asks, his lips following the trail of his palms. He looks up at me through his eyelashes. Tease!

"Yeah," I mumble, urging him with my hand. The tip of his tongue drags along the underside of my cock, and I groan. "Hunter!" He laughs, and takes me into his hot mouth, his tongue slithering over the vascular peaks and valleys. I arch my hips. *More, more, more!* I drag him to his feet and nip at his neck. I am careful; I don't want to frighten him. He gasps, but his hands roam over my chest. "I want to be inside of you," I growl. Again, my wolfishness threatens to overtake me. Hair prickles on my forearms, and my spine cracks. *Can he hear it?* "Hands on the wall, my love."

He does as I ask, and I kiss the hollow between his shoulder blades. Then, I kiss down the length of his spine, crouching so that I can press my teeth into the fatty, dimpled flesh of his ass. Hunter gasps, stiffening. I bit him too hard, his skin reddening. "Sorry."

"It's okay," he says. "I...liked it." Heat pools in my core. I fear I will cum without being touched, without touching him. I kiss the inflamed spot, then press my tongue against his puckered hole. He mewls. "Angus!" His voice is thick with longing. I rise and press the head of my cock inside of him. "Ah!"

"You feel so good," I groan as I slide in and out of him, reaching around his angular hip to stroke him. As my orgasm builds, my movements become more frenzied. *Careful,* I remind myself. I bite my lip, hard. The bones in my pelvis crack, and my spine elongates. *You'll scare him!*

Abruptly, Hunter cums, ropes of fluid trickling over my knuckles. I follow suit with a strangled howl.

I slump against him, my palm pressed against the wall beside him.

"Angus—"

I realize then that my hand isn't a hand so much as it is a paw. *Oh!* I reel back away from him. "I'm sorry."

He turns to look at me. I must look like a monster: a jumbled amalgamation of wolf and man. "Don't be sorry." Tentative, he touches my face. "I want to see you. All of you. Even the scary parts."

"You don't have to," I insist. *He will run from me.* My heart can't handle it. "I—" My teeth crowd my mouth, and the words die in my throat.

"I want to. Can you...show me?" He reaches for my hand, touching the rough pad on my palm. We both startle at the crunch of my knees as they reverse. It sounds like a gunshot and its ricochet. I can't seem to hold my wolfishness back. It's as though his express permission has quickened the process. I can't stop it.

Fur trickles down my spine, covering my chest in large swaths. Finally, my jaw snaps like a tree branch, forming a snout.

I step away from him, my heart pounding. My chest heaves as I catch my breath. Wolfish, his smell, and the smell of our lovemaking, overtakes me. It is intoxicating. I wish I could bury my muzzle in his armpit, and inhale. But he's going to run, isn't he? Of course,he will. I'm a monster. No one could love me.

Hunter reaches out and strokes my cheek. "I'm not scared," he says in a wobbly voice. Slowly, he wraps his arms around my broad shoulders, resting his cheek against my chest. Can he hear my heart hammering? "I don't want to go home to Geoff," he says, forlorn.

It is difficult to enunciate around my thick tongue. "Stay."

"They'll wonder where we are." They—Geoff and James, respectively. Carefully, so as to not inadvertently hurt him with one of my curved talons, I tilt his chin up. He looks at me unblinkingly, his lips parted.

"Stay," I insist.

"Come on." Naked, he leads me to an office, in which there is a desk covered in spreadsheets and a tangle of receipts. Unlike the rest of the backroom, this room is carpeted. I can't help but to imagine fucking him on that desk, his legs spread wide. But Hunter is tired. I gather him into my arms, delighting when he rubs his cheek against my fur. "You're so soft."

I laugh. The sound is bizarre, more like a cough. When he falls asleep, curled up against me, I close my eyes too.

In the morning, I wake in human form. Hunter's cheek is still on my chest, an arm thrown over my hip. We are a tangle of limbs, and my left arm, beneath him, is asleep. Despite the plush carpeting, the floor is hard and my back aches. I want to stretch, but I also don't want to disturb Hunter's slumber. He looks relaxed, whereas last night he looked pinched and somewhat sullen.

I crane my neck to look at the clock on his desk. *It's 4:45 a.m.*

I stroke his hair, brushing the unruly strands behind his ear. He stirs, but doesn't wake. I admire the naked knot of his thigh, slung over mine; the curve of his tilted hip; the softness of his belly. I kiss the crown of his head, lingering there. He smells like me. I touch the tooth mark on his neck from my kisses, the silvery scars of James' attack. Being with Hunter is a lesson in softness and taking care. He is so terribly fragile, a little porcelain lamb.

"What time is it?" Hunter murmurs, half asleep, his eyes still closed.

"Nearly five," I reply.

"I should get home," he says, cracking his eyelids. His green eyes meet mine. "Geoff will be worried." I had nearly forgotten about the extenuating circumstances that keep us from one another. The magic bubble bursts.

"Geoff can go fuck himself," I reply, tilting Hunters' chin to kiss him.

He grins against my lips, rising up on his palms so he can scoot closer. His tongue snakes into my mouth. When I slide my hand up his inner thigh, he snags my wrist in his hand.

"The last thing we need is for Geoff to find me here. With you." His lips brush against mine. "I don't know what this is—you and me—but I need to tell him it's over. It was a mistake to accept the ring, to let him back in the house."

I think of last night. *Hands on the wall, my love.* Neither of us acknowledged it. Maybe he thought it was in the heat of the moment. Maybe it was. But now, in the quiet of morning, when it is only he and I in the whole world, I want to say it again. "Hunter," I murmur, running my fingertips down his jawline. "I don't know what you want this to be. It doesn't have to be anything. But I need to tell you. I think that I'm in love with you."

"Me?" he asks, incredulous. It's as though the very thought is preposterous.

"Of course, you."

"But I'm not a were—"

I raise a hand to silence him. "I don't care what you are, Hunter. I care about *who* you are. I love you." The more I say it, the easier it gets, and the more I want to say it. The words dance on the tip of my tongue, tasting sweet.

He smiles. "I love you too, Angus."

It is time for us to go, but, instead, I pull him down on top of me. We can dawdle for five more minutes.

♦ ♦ ♦

We find most of our discarded clothes in the cafe proper. It's still dark out, but we don't turn the lights on. Hunter and I giggle when we bump hips or elbows. Just as I'm pulling my pants up over my ass, there is the scrape of a key and an influx of chilly morning air.

"What the *fuck*?" a voice exclaims. Hunter stiffens beside me, stumbling backward as if struck. It's Geoff, wearing pajama pants and a bomber jacket. He has a Maglite in hand and the beam blinds my eyes. I raise my hand to shield my face.

"You didn't come home," Geoff sniffs. "I was coming to check on you."

Hunter's shirt is still shucked up around his chest, and he pulls it down with shaking hands. He looks as though he's been slapped; his cheeks are a bright pink. "I—"

Geoff pulls something from his pocket. It's a revolver, and he holds it limply at his side. "Y'know, I didn't want to believe it."

"Geoff, why do you have that?" Hunter asks warily.

"You need it when you're hunting werewolves," Geoff replies, his eyes on me. "Isn't that right?"

"What are you talking about?" I ask. Adrenaline pours through me, making my heart race and palms sweat. Geoff aims the gun at my head, his finger resting on the trigger. The hair on the back of my neck prickles.

"Don't play dumb," he snaps. "At least give me that courtesy. Does Hunter know?"

Hunter is shaking, his eyes darting between two of us. "I'm sorry, Geoff," he whimpers. "I was wrong. I did a shitty thing. Please leave Angus out of it."

"You're right," Geoff says. "You did do a shitty thing. You've done a lot of shitty things recently, but this takes the fucking cake. But maybe you aren't seeing clearly right now."

I am running scenarios in my head. I can't transform and overtake him. Despite my strength, I am at my weakest when I am a muddle of shifting bone and knitting muscle, and he can shoot me before I get any traction on the hardwood floor. As a human I will be faster, but, still, I can't possibly outrun a bullet. So, instead, I bide my time and play dumb. "Werewolves?"

"What did I just fucking say?" Geoff shouts. His eyes are wide, red-rimmed; he clearly hadn't slept at all. "Don't patronize me."

"I'm not patronizing you. I just want to understand."
How does he know?

Geoff laughs, wiping his brow with the back of his gun hand. For a brief moment, the gun isn't trained on me, but it's short-lived. The gun returns to its position, aimed at the spot between my eyes. "I met your friend. The one with the stupid tattoos."

James.

Geoff continues, "He stopped by late last night. I was up, of course, waiting for my fiancé to come home." He cuts his eyes at Hunter, who looks sick. "He must have been waiting for *someone*, too. He told me everything. Showed me *everything*. Y'know, I brought this gun just to be safe. I hoped Hunter just fell asleep, paying the bills for the month. But what do I find? *You.*"

Hunter, tentative, steps toward Geoff. "Please let's just sit down and talk."

"Back the *fuck* up," Geoff says, turning the gun toward Hunter. The gun shakes in his grasp. Hunter gasps.

This is my chance. I lunge at Geoff, intending to wrestle him to the floor and disarm him. But he's quicker than I thought. *Bang!* The blast fills the space, and we all clap our hands over our ears. I can't help but to think of Geoff stomping on my knee. *Had he done it again?* My stomach hurts.

"Angus!" I slowly turn to look at Hunter, whose freckles are crimson. Red is not his color. I want to tell him so, but I can't seem to get my mouth to work. Everything feels too heavy. Why does everything feel so heavy? I would very much like to lay down.

My legs crumple and I land heavily on my butt. "Oh god, Angus." Hunter falls to his knees beside me, and I want to tell him to get up. Geoff has a gun, you stupid man. Hunter presses his palm against my abdomen and pain ricochets through me.

I'm bleeding. Blood trickles from between Hunter's fingers. "Oh," I say, finding my voice. "I've been shot." My eyes feel heavy, and I close them. *This feels better.*

"Wake up, *Angus*!" Hunter says. I force my eyes open. I'm lying on my back now. *How did I get here?*

"I'm tired," I mumble.

"I know, baby," Hunter says. "Stay with me, okay?" It sounds like he's underwater. I can feel his words reverberating through my skull, and I want to tell him he'll drown.

"Get the fuck up, Hunter," Geoff says.

"Geoff, if I let go, he'll die." Hunter replies, crying. "You'll be a murderer. Is that what you want?"

I want to sleep. Their voices fade as I close my eyes.

CHAPTER EIGHTEEN
(JAMES)

———◁◆▷———

I t had felt good — being with Angus again. His body felt familiar, like putting on the winter jacket that's been in the closet for nine months. All I had to say was *I'm sorry*. It was like magic. I was sorry, then he was half-naked in a bathroom stall. I was sorry and he took my hand on the walk home. I was sorry and we laid together on the lumpy mattress, naked, sharing a cigarette. I didn't even have to apologize for any of the things I'm *not* sorry about, namely, Nedry.

I thought we would be back together. But he wasn't in bed when I woke up. When I tried to touch him when we crossed paths, he would shake his head. *That night was a mistake,* he said morosely, shrugging off my questions for weeks. We stopped sharing a bed altogether. More often than not, he would sleep in the hammock out back, his long legs dangling. He's clearly still hung up on that human.

I wake to the sun high in the sky. It's mid-afternoon, and the house is quiet, save for some shuffling and

Chapter Eighteen (james)

hushed murmurs in the kitchen. I roll over, reaching for the pack of cigarettes and the lighter I had left on the armrest of the pullout couch. I'm not supposed to smoke indoors, but I light one anyway. The nicotine makes me alert, and, more importantly, it laps against the pleasure centers in my brain. I know it's artificial, but, right now, it's all I have. Fucking Angus in that stinking bathroom stall was the last good feeling I've had, and that was weeks ago, now.

Ama appears in the doorway to the kitchen, leaning heavily against the doorframe. "Come here," she says. Her face is impassive, save for a tic that makes her ear twitch.

Each time I see her, I swear she's got a new wrinkle traversing her cheeks, the baggy skin under her eyes, and highlighting her perpetual frown.

I groan. I imagine she has something for me to fix. I have become the Finder of Things and the Fixer of Gadgets. I've become particularly adept at reprogramming the microwave when the clock blinks *12:00, 12:00, 12:00*. Or she wants to bitch at me about the cigarettes.

"Now," Ama snaps.

With an exaggerated sigh, I slip on the jeans I discarded the night before. When I follow her into the kitchen, she wordlessly jabs at the television screen with one spindly finger. The volume is muted, but closed captions crawl along the bottom of the screen. It's apparent why she has summoned me:

[The search for the person of interest, James Volkov, continues. Police are...].

My likeness appears on screen. It's grainy, taken from a security camera and blown up tenfold. I'm smiling, my arm draped around the late Ronald Nedry III. Ronnie's head is tilted toward mine, his mouth open, mid-sentence. I honestly can't recall anything he said. I can't even remember the sound of his voice. But I do remember how he tasted. Sometimes, I dream about it. In the photograph, we're outdoors; it must have been taken while we were walking to his car.

Shit. My bowels turn to water. Without preamble, Ama turns off the television and says, "You need to go." *The words I've been secretly dreading.*

"I can't just *go*. It's not that fucking simple." Suddenly, I am cognizant of the proverbial noose around my neck. It tightens as I speak. "They're looking for me." My voice shakes. I hate to admit it, but I'm rattled. I feel boxed in, trapped in a snare of barbed wire.

"Don't curse at me, pup. It is that simple—*leave*. I don't care what you do from there."

"I need to talk to Angus, Lei—"

She cuts me off. "No, you don't. You need to walk out the back door without a single *word*. Not one. I want you to be miles away before they even *think* about you."

"They're my pack," I say, indignant. I'm tired of being bossed around by an old woman. She's insignificant. I could eat her, then use her bones as toothpicks.

"It's Angus' pack, if I recall," she replies smugly.

"Listen, you old bitch!" I take a step toward her, and her eyes narrow. Then, with nary a word, Ama moves faster than I even thought possible. Before I can even comprehend what is happening, her small hands are laced around my throat. She squeezes tight, and I can only wheeze. I try to push her away, but she's as immovable as if she's rooted to the floor. *How?*

"Pack your things," she barks, "and *go*." Finally, she releases me. Her semi-lupine ears swivel.

The thought of walking out without Leigh feels like ripping asunder. My stomach churns. I can't go without my twin. "Ama," I beg. "I can't—"

"You will," she replies coolly. "You upended their lives. They are all happy here. What must they do to stay with you? Live in the woods? Sneak across border crossings?" She shakes her head. "I won't let you do that."

"It's not your decision."

"You're right. It's not. But I've fed you, clothed you, and my rules were clear. You've broken them more than once, and you forced them to break those same rules."

"I didn't make anyone do anything," I snort, indignant.

"Leigh and Luka offered up that human on a silver platter for you, just because you asked. I saw them both, afterward. It wrecked them." I don't remember much about that night. As soon as Angus bested me, I started drinking, drowning my sorrows. Within the hour, I was floating somewhere near the ceiling, my eyes blurry and my tongue loose. I only recall waking up on the kitchen floor, the linoleum cool under my cheek, my mouth tasting like vomit and stale beer.

Still, I argue with her. "They're fine."

"You do realize that Luka is barely ever here, right?" She crosses her arms over her chest. "He can't bear to be around you. He can't face Angus."

"He's fine," I snap. "I'll leave, but not without them."

"You'll leave in a body bag then," she says smoothly. I guffaw.

What an overconfident cunt! I move to pass her, but she places her palm against my chest, driving me backward. I clench my jaw.

"Move," I growl.

She snorts, her nostrils flaring.

When she doesn't oblige, I step into my wolfishness, my eyes never leaving her inscrutable facade. My body is nearly too large for the space. I must hunch over.

Slowly, her jaw contorts and elongates to accommodate a snout. Her fur erupts from her flesh; it's white, like Angus', though it's more of an ivory shade, yellowed by age. She's skinny, each rib defined and her shoulder blades sticking out at seemingly impossible angles. Ama pulls her lips away from her teeth in a snarl.

I leap at her, and she swipes at my snout. Her nails leave shallow, bloodless scratches behind. I laugh and drop my shoulder, catching her in the stomach and lifting her off her feet. She yelps and careens into the kitchen counter, the drying rack crashing to the floor and scattering dishes everywhere. As soon as she regains her feet, she lunges at me, jaws gnashing. She is a whirling dervish of claw and tooth, but I parry each attack as it comes. She's old, and weak.

Pathetic, really.

When I close my jaws around her throat, Ama kicks my stomach with her back legs. It's not quite enough to knock the breath out of me, but, for the briefest moment, I am disarmed. Somehow, she rolls out from under me, palms my snout, and slams me sideways into the wall. I try to scrabble away, but she doesn't release me. It's as though she's gained the strength of three wolves.

"That's the problem with you pups," she growls. "You don't respect your elders. Now, get out of my house."

"Fine," I growl. "Fine!" When she releases me, my fur melts away and I give her a poisonous look. "They'll come looking for me. You can't stop them."

"They won't," she says confidently. "Bye-bye now."

I smoke a cigarette while strolling along the shoreline, searching for my sister. A cold sweat trickles down my spine, wetting my armpits. Despite the rapidly encroaching sunset, I find her near the pier, sunning herself on a lounger

She pushes her sunglasses up onto the crown of her head when she spots me, squinting. "Get up," I tell her. "We're leaving."

"What are you talking about?" she asks, wrinkling her button nose. She stretches out her long legs, burnished by the sun. "A 'hello, nice to see you' would have been nice."

"The cops know who I am," I reply, gathering up her towels and sunscreen, tossing her sandy flip-flops onto her lap. "Where are the others?"

"Stop!" Leigh snaps. "Slow down. What do you mean?" She reaches for her coverup, pulling the thin fabric around her shoulders.

I grit my teeth, trying to tamp down my frustration. I clench my fists, my nails cutting half-moons into my palms. *Sometimes, she's infuriating.* "Just tell me where Angus and Luka are."

"They said they would hang out in town and then go out to eat. I didn't want to go." She slips on her shoes. "Let's just go to Ama's. They'll probably be back soon."

"I can't," I huff. "Ama kicked me out. The Portland cops know my name, it's all over the news." I'm starting to feel paranoid. Every pedestrian who meets my eye recognizes me. Every phone call is to Crime Stoppers. Every conversation starts with *is that the guy from TV?*

"Shit," Leigh breathes. To her credit, she starts to gather her things, her hands shaking.

"Go pack some things," I tell her, already striding away. "I'll find the others."

Seconds later, as if by kismet, I nearly collide with Luka, a plastic container stuffed with cheesecake in his hand. "Where's Angus?" I snap.

"I don't know, man," he mumbles, looking at his sneakers. *Liar.* I grasp the younger man's arm, squeezing tight. If we weren't in public, if I wasn't trying to be incognito, I would shake him until the words rattled from him.

"Tell me, pup," I growl. "I'm not in the mood." When he looks at me, startled, I bare my teeth. "Now," I add, none too nicely. He winces, clutching his takeout container. I'm woefully unprepared for the answer. When I hear the human's name, the ground spins beneath my feet.

CHAPTER
NINETEEN (HUNTER)

—◁◆▷—

"Get *up*," Geoff repeats, impatient. It's as though the man standing before me isn't Geoff at all, but a tulpa made up to look like him. Geoff was always distant and self-serving, but never cruel.

I shake my head, unable to tear my eyes away from Angus' face. His own eyes are closed, and as much as I beg, he won't open them again. "Get up or I'll shoot you in the fucking head," Geoff threatens, pressing the gun barrel against my temple. My insides turn to liquid.

"I can't," I whisper.

Geoff kicks me in the ribs, and I yelp.

Despite the pain in my side, I don't take my hands off the wet mess that is Angus' stomach. *Don't die, don't die, don't die.* I can't seem to staunch the river of blood, not entirely. Tributaries trickle between my fingers, soaking my hands and forearms.

"Now," Geoff insists. He grabs the collar of my shirt, towing me upward. Forced to my feet, Angus' wound will bleed unabated. *Don't you dare die!*

"What's your plan?" I ask Geoff, wiping Angus' blood off my face with the back of my hand. It smears, getting into my mouth and nose. "Did you expect me to just go home with you?"

"You aren't coming home," Geoff says, training the gun on me. "As soon as I got here, found you and that monster, I knew none of us were."

"What do you mean?" I ask. Geoff shifts his weight from foot to foot, as if imbued with a manic energy he can't quite control. He looks like a wild animal caught in a trap, driven insane by his circumstances.

"I'm not going to jail," Geoff says, his voice wobbling over the word *jail*. "This is all your fault," he continues. "I didn't come here to do this. I came here to bring you home. I thought he was lying—"

"He's going to die," I sob, looking down at Angus.

His flesh is a splotchy gray, and he is absolutely soaked in blood. It pools on the floor, covering the spot where, as a bored teenager, I scratched a heart into the wood with a pocket knife. I got into so much trouble when my parents found it.

"He's not even a person. I've just put down a dog." He is trying to convince himself of something. It is apparent in the way his words tumble over one another, and his brow furrows into taut mounds. Is he grappling with guilt?

"I love him," I say, whirling on my fiancé. I'm angry, too angry to care that there's a loaded gun between the two of us. I jab my finger against the hard edge of his sternum. "I don't even fucking *like* you anymore."

Geoff snorts, his nostrils flaring. "Yeah, you've made that very *clear*."

Suddenly, there's a smash and we are bombarded with pieces of broken glass. We both duck, throwing our arms over our heads in a feeble attempt to protect our eyes. A loud snarl accompanies the tumult. I peek through my fingers and find three hulking shapes, so large they block the streetlights. Three wolf-people advance on Geoff and me, and Geoff turns the gun on them.

"Step away from our Alpha," one of the creatures growl. It is the smallest of the three, gray with a strikingly black muzzle. It's as though it has dipped its face in ink. The voice is somewhat feminine. And despite the timbre, I recognize it—*Leigh*. Geoff isn't sure where to aim the gun. He sweeps it back and forth. "Drop it," Leigh commands. Geoff doesn't do as she says, and the she-wolf springs.

Her jaws clamp on his forearm. When she wrenches it, the gun clatters to the ground, skittering under the counter. Geoff screams as she flings him like a rag doll, and he hits the ground with a resounding thud. He whimpers, pulling his knees into his chest and wrapping his arms around them. He doesn't attempt to get up.

"I've been waiting *so long* to do this," a grey, mottled wolf says, turning his attention to me. It's James. He bares his teeth, clearly relishing this moment. His breath is malodorous, reminiscent of the alley when it rains. "You're going to taste *so good*."

"Fuck you!" I exclaim, clenching my fists tight. I'm surprised by my own outburst. I'm terrified. Nausea rolls over me, threatening to fold me in half.

Chapter Nineteen (hunter)

The wolves are three times my size, and I feel as though I'm looking up at the apex of a great wave, threatening to shove me into the ocean's darkest depths. I am suddenly very cognizant of my breath. *In. Out. In, out, in, out, inout, inout.*

"You're dangerous," James barks. The ground shifts under my feet. *No!* I want to shout. "You did this," he continues, advancing on me. "You're the reason Angus is dying."

"I didn't. I love—"

James pauses mid-step. "What did you say?"

"I love him." My voice is remarkably steady.

James' eyes narrow, and his ears pin back against his skull. "Angus is mine," he spits. His lips pull back from his yellowing teeth in a deranged smile. "Say 'good bye,' Hunter."

When he pounces, something large knocks him off-balance. He slides on his belly across the slick, blood-smeared floor. James' skull strikes the edge of the counter, and a strangled yip escapes him before he lays still, dazed.

Angus, wolfish, stands in front of me, his large paw clasped against his still-bleeding abdomen. His chest heaves, a bizarre whistling sound accompanying each breath. "The rest of you, go home." Each utterance is a struggle, but we hang onto every word. It's some sort of power he is imbued with as Alpha. Neither I, nor the wolves, move until he's done speaking and his knees buckle beneath him.

"Angus!" I wrap my arms around his thick neck, trying, in vain, to pull him to his feet. But he's too heavy.

"The gun, Hunter," Angus prompts. I scan the room, searching for the weapon. I can just barely see the curve of the pommel beneath the counter. It catches the light. "Leigh, Luka, get the fuck out of here," he adds.

On the floor, James groans, struggling to regain his feet. Blood oozes from a gash above his eye. "I will kill your human pet," he mutters. "You've been so pathetic since you met."

"If you touch him, I'll do what I should have done a long time ago," Angus replies haltingly. "It's my fault. I shouldn't have let you live this long."

James laughs humorlessly. He uses the counter to haul himself upright. "You don't have the nerve," he spits. "You never have." He lunges at Angus, and Angus rises to meet him. The two wolves clash in a cacophony of snarls and yips. It is difficult to tell who is whom; they are merely a dervish of fur and teeth. When they separate, James is gurgling, blood pouring from his throat, a crimson wave. He crumples into a heap.

James!" Leigh howls. She rushes at Angus, biting at his throat. But his long mane tempers the attack, and he slashes at her with his claws. She yips. Then, Luka follows suit, his teeth sinking into Angus' shoulder. Angus, already weak, is easily overpowered by his packmates.

"What are you doing?" I scream. He's their Alpha, but their allegiance lies with James. I can't fathom why. He's a cold-blooded monster, driven by his own whims. He doesn't strike me as someone who deserves blind devotion, especially when juxtaposed with Angus Chilton. The latter is kind, trustworthy, deserving of love.

I don't care what you are...I love you, he'd said.

I tear my eyes away, running for the gun. It's under the counter, and I can barely touch the barrel with my fingertips. I curse, and search for something to grab it with. A broom, knocked over in the fray, is very near James' crumpled form.

With only a second of hesitation, I run for it. James grabs my ankle, pulling me down. My chin strikes the ground and I see stars. Managing to close a hand on the broom handle, I swing it at his head, hitting him in the snout. When he yelps and releases me, I scrabble to the counter on hands and knees, shoving the broom beneath it. In one fluid motion, I bat the gun out and grab it, pulling back the hammer. Whirling, I aim at the three fighting wolves.

Angus is on his back, slashing and kicking at his pack mates.

"Stop!" I scream, pulling the trigger. I've never shot a gun before, and the recoil forces my hand up. The bullet buries itself in the far wall, just beyond the wolves. Shit. I aim again and pull the trigger. But the chamber is empty. I pull the trigger again and again, in disbelief. *Click, click, click. We are going to die here,* I think. The wolves will kill Angus, then Geoff and I for fun. It'll be like shooting fish in a barrel. Angus is the only thing keeping me alive right now.

Angus bats the two wolves away, a veritable roar emanating from him. They hesitate, ears pinned back against their skulls. He is, after all, their Alpha; he surely has some sort of hold over them, even now.

"Submit," he growls. "Or I'll kill you." Luka whines, taking a step back, ducking his head. Leigh, however, doesn't move. "Leigh!" Angus warns.

James rises to his feet. "Leave my sister be," he manages around his ravaged throat.

"Leave the humans be," Angus counters.

Again, the two males clash, and tear at one another. Angus, finally, overtakes his former mate. He straddles him, holding his shoulders down with his paws. With his arms still free, James sinks his fist into Angus' gunshot wound. Angus howls in pain, and bites James' throat. James' blood, flowing freely, is staunched by Angus' jaws as he squeezes.

"You're killing him," Leigh screams. "Angus, stop!"

But Angus isn't listening. He squeezes tighter. James tears at Angus' shoulders in a vain attempt to get free. Then, with a great heave, Angus breaks James' neck. The crunch of bone makes me heave, and I retch onto the floor. Leigh's fur melts away and she runs toward her twin, sobbing.

"Jay!" Angus steps away, watching as Leigh throws her body onto her brother's wolven chest, slapping at his cheeks as though she can rouse him. "Please wake up, Jay."

Slowly, James' fur melts away, and his naked, human body emerges. His eyes — unblinking, unseeing — are fixed on the ceiling, his head bent at a grotesque angle.

Leigh strokes his hair. "Wake up, wake up, please."

Angus turns to look at Luka, who has also stepped out of his fur. The younger man averts his eyes, embarrassed. He wipes snot from his nose, silent pink tears trickling down his cheeks. Angus scans the room with tired eyes, slumping to the floor when he finds me safe and sound. I rush to him, trying, in vain, to support his weight and help him regain his feet.

"Hunter," he murmurs. I settle for cradling his large head on my lap.

"I need to call for an ambulance," I tell him. My eyes are watery, and I blink the tears away over, and over, and over again. I can't seem to stop crying. Across the room, Leigh's sobs have escalated into wails.

Luka, unmoving, watches as I take out my phone. "Wait," he says. "Please. We need to get James out of here."

"I don't give a *fuck* about James," I snap, jabbing at the screen.

"Listen," Luka pleads. "If James is here when the police arrive, it'll expose us. Angus will get into trouble. Hunter, please. Wait five minutes." I clench my jaw tight, my nostrils flaring. Luka is right. If James is found, Angus will be tethered to a hospital bed, handcuffs biting into his wrists.

"Go," I concede, my thumb hovering above the CALL button. Angus' eyes are closed now, and his breathing is ragged. I stroke the fur of his muzzle with my free hand.

"We need to go, Leigh," Luka tells his packmate, hauling her to her feet. She sags in his arms, her face contorted in abject sorrow. "I'll carry Jay." Luka transforms in fits and starts, his bones crunching. In the quiet room, the sound echoes. Panting, Luka lifts James' body over his shoulder. He glances at me. "Thank you."

He walks gingerly through the broken glass and out of the cafe, Leigh wordlessly trailing behind.

I make the call. While we wait, I bury my nose in Angus' fur. "Help is coming," I tell him. "I know everything hurts so badly, I know. But please, I need you to change back. Angus, can you hear me?"

✦ ✦ ✦

The hospital lobby is cold. Gooseflesh peppers my skin, and I rub absently at my arms. The stitches on my forehead tug, but the pain doesn't quite register. Angus has been in surgery for hours. I try to eavesdrop on the conversations at the nurse's station, but they've only talked about their plans for the weekend; what so-and-so's kid got into trouble for at school; and how bitchy the Charge Nurse has been today.

I get up for my fourth cup of coffee, slotting two quarters into the machine. I didn't have any money, but a kind elderly woman put a handful of change into my hand. *You look like you're about to fall over,* she'd said, *get a sandwich in the cafeteria.* Instead, I drink cup after cup of stale coffee, waiting, bladder bursting.

Despite the caffeine, I keep dozing, chin to chest. I must have fallen asleep again because I am startled when a woman touches my arm. She is dressed in surgical garb, a smear of red on the lapel. "Mr. Bailey?"

"Yeah," I reply, shooting out of my chair. The blood rushing to my extremities makes me dizzy. "How is he?"

"Mr. Chilton will be okay," she says. "He'll need a few days in the ICU, but we were able to remove all of the bullet fragments."

"Can I see him?"

"He'll be asleep for a few hours, but I can take you back." She beckons, and I follow her through the labyrinth of halls, toward a suite. Inside, Angus lays supine on the bed, the blanket pulled up to his chin. A machine beeps in the rhythm of his heart; it is even and strong. I rush to his side, pulling up a chair. "A nurse will arrive shortly to check on him," the surgeon says, before heading off to her next patient.

I reach for Angus' hand, kissing his knuckles. "Everything will be okay," I tell him, even though I'm not entirely sure that's true. Geoff was apprehended. James is dead. Leigh and Luka ran. "*You* will be okay," I amend.

A soft knock on the open door draws my attention. It's a diminutive woman, her face lined with wrinkles. She wears a coat and knit cap pulled down around her ears. I recognize her, having seen her shuffling along Bird's Nest or sitting like a gargoyle on her porch — Ama Chilton. "How is he?" she asks without preamble.

"He'll be okay," I reply. "The surgeon said he will be in the hospital for a while, but he'll be okay."

The old woman pushes a chair next to mine, the legs screeching against the linoleum floor. She sits, patting Angus' leg. "Luka told me what happened." I think of the young man, harried, his lower lip trembling as fur sprouted over his abdomen. He tenderly hefted James' body over his shoulder, covering the man's nakedness with his forearm. It's as though he

wanted to give James some dignity. Despite everything, I can't bring myself to be angry at Luka. He's
just a kid.

"You know," Ama murmurs. "I think that I was
wrong about you."

"About me?" I ask hesitantly.

"You, yes—humans, in general. I told Angus that
you couldn't handle it. I thought it would break you.
I thought that being with you would break *him*, too.
But," she rests her cool hand atop mine. "I was wrong."

I don't know what to say, so I don't say anything
at all. "You're good for him, I think," she continues.
She turns to look at me, her cerulean eyes large and
glaringly bright, despite the murky cataracts clouding
her pupils. "Do you love him?"

"Yes," I murmur. "I love him." I feel as though I'm
sharing a secret. Sharing it with her makes it more real,
somehow. Ama nods sagely.

"What happens now?" I ask.

"That's up to you and Aggie, isn't it?" I can't help
but to chuckle at the sweet nickname. "He's an Alpha
without a pack. And, he's a man who has lost more than
his fair share." She smiles at her grandson's supine
form, his chest rising and falling. "But, he has you."

"He does," I assure her.

She rises and leans over to kiss Angus on the forehead. "I'll leave him in your capable hands."

EPILOGUE
(ANGUS)

———⊲◆⊳———

W harton in wintertime is cold and damp. The sea grass becomes stiff with snow, and my joints become stiff, too. I try, in vain, to stretch the taut muscles in my neck by turning this way and that. Hunter and I walk arm-in-arm to Ebb and Flow. He needs to open the cafe, and I need a cup of coffee. My body is still slow, and Hunter is careful to keep my pace, walking in-step.

"Nearly there," he encourages.

I huff, my hot breath condensing into a mist. "I know where it is."

"You're cranky in the morning," Hunter observes with a chuckle. His nose is pink with cold and I long to kiss it.

When we reach Main Street, then the cafe, he slips out from under my arm to unlock the door. The renovations were completed last week, and it's still a surprise when the lights come on. The wall that Hunter shot, and was damaged by James' bulk, has been replaced with birch shiplap. The floor had been pulled up and replaced, too. Hunter couldn't get the blood out no matter how much he scrubbed and cursed and scrubbed some more. Behind the counter, all of the mugs made by Geoff are gone, replaced with vintage finds pilfered from Ama's kitchen.

"Let me get you some coffee," Hunter says, kissing me. His cold nose touches mine.

"Please." I ease into a chair, pressing my palm against my still sore abdomen. The muscles therein aren't quite what they used to be. I can't help but to think of James whenever my body aches. As much as I'd like to feel otherwise, his death was a tragedy. It fundamentally changed me. Everything about that morning had. The only port in the tumultuous sea was Hunter Bailey and his lovely green eyes.

I wake suddenly, thrashing at enemies unseen. "Hey, hey," Hunter soothes, grasping my arms. "Angus, you're in the hospital." With effort, I crack open my eyes to find him smiling down at me, a bandage affixed to his forehead. My tongue sticks to the roof of my mouth, and I gesture for water. He reaches for a cup on the nearby table, slipping the straw between my dry lips. The water is refreshing. I think that it might be the best water I've ever tasted. It washes away the taste of my blood, his blood, their blood.

James. *"He's dead, isn't he?" I croak. My voice sounds far away. It's as though I'm floating, entirely separate from this body, this room, this town, this reality. I think that I like floating up here, borne upward by wings made of oxycodone. Still, I am very aware that this feeling is temporary. It's an ache deep*

*in my core. Soon, the tethers of reality will ensnare
me, dragging me back to the cold, hard hospital bed.*

*Hunter sits on the edge of the bed, clasping my
hand tight. "Yeah," he murmurs. "Leigh and Luka
took him away." A sob bubbles up before I can tamp it
down. Without a word, Hunter lays beside me, careful
not to touch my hurting body or the various tubes and
wires draped over and into me. He kisses my cheek,
wiping away the fast-rolling tears. "I'm so sorry. I'm
so, so sorry." I swear that if I am very still, I can
still feel James' vertebrae breaking between my teeth.
I bury my face in the curve of Hunter's neck, crying
like a child.*

Hunter brews a pot of coffee for me while opening
up shop. When it's done, he pours a generous helping
into my favorite mug. It's white, with little blue daisies
around the rim. When I was an adolescent, Ama would
fill it with a splash of coffee and a generous helping of
cream so that I would feel grown up.

"Stay," I say before Hunter can head back behind
the counter. I pull him down onto my lap. "Stay."

"We open in half an hour," he says, playfully swatting at my arm. "Behave."

"If I ever agree to that, shoot me again," I
deadpan. He squirms on my lap but doesn't rise. I've
ensnared him.

"You're incorrigible," he says laughingly, but he
kisses me.

"Just awful." I agree. I deepen the kiss, slipping my
tongue into his mouth. Hunter tastes like wintergreen
toothpaste. I must, too. This morning, we brushed our
teeth at the same bathroom sink. I remember winking

at his reflection, making him laugh and dribble tooth-paste down his chin. Staying at his bungalow has been a godsend. When I dream of James and wake up with my eyes swollen, Hunter kisses my wet cheeks and holds me tight. He takes my hands and anchors me when my guilt—and grief—threatens to overtake me. *You couldn't have saved him,* he soothes.

I can't help but to think of the backroom, only a few feet away. We could be through the door in a breath, and I could be inside of him in two. "Half an hour?" I confirm.

"You know we open at 7," Hunter snorts.

The bell above the door rings as Renee and María enter, both bleary-eyed. "God, get a room," Renee says, wrinkling her nose. But she smiles too. Renee is happy that Hunter is happy, and as a result, he's been freeing up the reins.

"I want to," I growl into Hunter's ear, so only he can hear.

He blushes and slides off my lap. "I need to go get the cash drawer sorted," he says. "Can you guys finish setting up?" He looks down at me. "Drink your coffee, Aggie."

I roll my eyes, swatting at his ass. He loves my grandmother's nickname for me. Hunter pushes through the swinging door and I take a sip of my coffee. The girls chat amongst themselves, finishing the tasks Hunter had started before I distracted him with my roving hands.

Candy walks in, bundled in a heavy, bell-sleeved cardigan. "Hey," she says to her coworkers, and by extension, me. Our relationship is tenuous at best, though she's warming up to me. She only wants to protect her brother. Candy sits at my table, crossing her legs. "Guess who I talked to last night?"

"Julian?" I ask, referring to her on-and-off boyfriend.

"I'm not talking to Julien right now. He's being an asshole. *Geoff.* His sentencing is next week. He's doing really well, all things considered." She looks at me expectantly as if waiting for a response.

But I don't have one. He is guilty of attempted murder, and rightfully so. *A lover's quarrel rocks Wharton,* the Wharton Gazette exclaimed.

"I'm glad he has you," I tell Candy. I'm happy Geoff survived the ordeal, but I have no interest in speaking to him, or about him.

Candy glances at the clock. "I'd better go get my apron and clock in. See you in a few."

"I was just about to go check on Hunter," I say. I rise, padding into the back. Candy disappears into the employee restroom. Emmanuel gives me a brief nod, up to his elbows in flour. Hunter is in the office, the door ajar. He's humming, as he does when he's alone and concentrating on something. I saunter in, grinning like the cat who ate the canary. "Go back out front," Hunter says, pushing his reading glasses up the bridge of his nose. "I'll only be a minute."

I lean against the desk next to him. "I think—" I gently take the pen out of his hand, setting it aside. "I think that I would like to do something I've been thinking about for a while."

"And what's that?"

"Fucking you on this desk," I reply, fisting the front of his shirt and pulling him to his feet in one fluid motion. I shuck his shirt over his head, peppering his neck with kisses. His stubble tickles my lips.

"I've got to get to work," Hunter murmurs, but his eyes are already half-lidded, little whimpers escaping his parted lips. "We open in—"

I hush him, unbuttoning his jeans and letting the fabric pool around his ankles. Hunter steps out of them obediently. His cock is already hard, tenting his boxer briefs. I stroke it gently through the fabric until his hips begin to buck. I lightly nibble at his neck, quickly freeing myself from my own pants and underwear, my turgid cock at full attention. I lick the curve of Hunter's ear, sucking his earlobe between my teeth. "Suck."

Hunter shivers in delight at the command. He drops to his knees, opening his mouth wide for me, tongue lolling. Painstakingly slowly, I press into his mouth, groaning when my head presses against his soft palate. I slowly rock into and out of his mouth, cupping the back of his head with a firm hand. His eyes flutter closed. "You look so gorgeous," I tell him, pressing into his mouth until his nose touches my pubic bone. His tongue slithers over the underside of my cock as his face reddens. Finally, I release him, and he gasps for air, drool wetting his chin.

I push all of the administrivia on the desk aside. A stapler and a pencil sharpener hit the ground with a crash. Papers flutter like seagulls heading home to roost. Hunter winces. "I just organized all of that."

"I'll reorganize it for you, love," I reply, crushing his mouth with mine. Our teeth clack together, and we both chuckle. I squeeze his ass, popping him up onto the desk. "This is exactly what I pictured," I tell him, spreading his legs wide. "You. Just like this." I suck my finger into my mouth, wetting it with saliva. Then, I press the digit against his puckered hole, easing it inside of him. He gasps, tilting his head back in pleasure. He reaches between his legs to stroke his cock, and we work in tandem, driving him toward orgasm. Hunter's eyes shut tight, his parted lips releasing shallow breaths that sound like *yes, yes, yes*. I gently slip a second finger inside and he strokes himself more quickly.

"Oh god, Angus," he moans. "I'm right there."

Slowly, I pull my fingers out, replacing them with my exuberant cock. Being gentle is torture, but I've learned how to butt up against his very limit without breaking him. If he weren't human, we could rut unabashedly like animals—biting, growling, gentleness cast aside in favor of savage desire. Hunter moans, grasping the curve of my hip with his free hand. I prop his legs up on my shoulders, thrusting into and out of him. The desk rocks, striking the wall with resounding thuds. Someone will surely hear, but I don't care.

"I want you to cum for me, baby," I tell him.

"Oh!" His body stiffens, his ass gripping my cock tight. Thick ropes of his own cum splatter against his belly. His eyes roll into his head as the pleasure overtakes him. "Angus—!"

I resume thrusting, desperate to cum, too. I can feel the wolfish part of me threatening to come out, but I temper the impulse. It doesn't frighten Hunter, but I can't kiss him with a snout nor grasp his hips tight without human hands. Nostrils flaring, I lean over him, hand on the desktop. Finally, an orgasm shakes me, and I cum deeply inside of him. "God," I groan, nearly collapsing atop him. "You're so good, love."

He strokes my hair. "You're not so bad yourself."

Suddenly, there's a knock on the door. "Hey love-birds, shop's open," Renee says. "There's a line of customers down to the pier." We laugh. We won't see more than three customers all day, not in Wharton in wintertime.

"Let's get to work," I whisper, kissing his throat.

"Stay," he says instead.

♦ ♦ ♦

END.

ACKNOWLEDGMENTS

I want to thank my family for buying me a word processor when I was in middle school; Carleigh, for everything and then some; Tatum West, for teaching me everything I know; Reddhott Covers, for this gorgeous cover; and the powerful, magical women at 4 Horsemen for believing in me and this story.

ABOUT THE AUTHOR
BEAU LAKE

<◁◆▷>

B eau Lake is a tattooed, blue-haired, queer romance writer skulking around the mountains of Virginia. She is very happily married and lives with a menagerie of children (2), dogs (3), and plants.

Her current hobbies include digital art, social/animal activism, and screaming into the void. Mostly the latter. She is passionate about ending greyhound racing in the United States and worldwide, and shares her home with a retired racer named River. Other favorite activities include listening to true crime podcasts, staring at empty Word documents while having existential crises, and asking herself "What Would Stephen King Do?"

Beau writes both traditional and horror/supernatural LGBTQIA romance. Werewolves are her favorite because they have sharp teeth and even sharper personalities.

Some of her published work includes the well-received DC Pride series, co-written with Tatum West

(Proud, Out, and The Space Between Us). The Wolves of Wharton is her first supernatural series, with more to come!

She can be found online via Facebook, Twitter, or at authorbeaulake.com. She loves t3alking with readers and can be reached at authorbeaulake@gmail.com. Vegetarian recipes are also appreciated.

facebook.com/beau.lake.77
facebook.com/groups/1813967932089935
Twitter @beau__lake
beaulakebooks.com

OTHER BOOKS

Co-authored w/ Tatum West:
Proud, Out, The Space Between Us

BY BEAU LAKE:

The Beast Beside Me
The Beast Within Me

4 Horsemen Publications

Romance

Emily Bunney
All or Nothing
All the Way
All She Needs
Having it All
All at Once
All Together
All for Her

Mimi Francis
Private Lives
Second Chances

Fantasy/Paranormal Romance

Blaise Ramsay
Through The Black Mirror
The City of Nightmares
The Astral Tower
The Lost Book of the Old Blood
Shadow of the Dark Witch
Chamber of the Dead God

Valerie Willis
Cedric: The Demonic Knight
Romasanta: Father of Werewolves
The Oracle: Keeper of the Gaea's Gate
Artemis: Eye of Gaea
King Incubus: A New Reign

J.M. Paquette
Klauden's Ring
Solyn's Body
The Inbetween
Hannah's Heart
Call Me Forth
Invite Me In

V.C. Willis
Prince's Priest
Priest's Assassin

Young Adult Fantasy

C.R. Rice
Denial
Anger
Bargaining
Depression
Acceptance

J.B. Moonstar
Russ and The Hidden Voice
Taylor and the Red Wolf Rescue
Jenna and the Legend of the White Wolf
Jenna and the Return of the White Wolf
Jan and the Chinese Crested Tern Rescue

4HorsemenPublications.com